ELENA KNOWS

First published by Charco Press 2021
Charco Press Ltd., Office 59, 44-46 Morningside Road, Edinburgh
EH10 4BF

Copyright © Claudia Piñeiro 2007
Published by arrangement with Schavelzon Graham Agencia Literaria
www.schavelzongraham.com

First published in Spanish as *Elena sabe* by Alfaguara (Argentina)
English translation copyright © Frances Riddle 2021

The rights of Claudia Piñeiro to be identified as the author of this work and
of Frances Riddle to be identified as the translator of this work have been
asserted by them in accordance with the Copyright, Designs and Patents Act
1988.

Work published with funding from the 'Sur' Translation Support Programme
of the Ministry of Foreign Affairs of Argentina / Obra editada en el marco
del Programa 'Sur' de Apoyo a las Traducciones del Ministerio de Relaciones
Exteriores y Culto de la República Argentina.

A CIP catalogue record for this book is available from the British Library.

ISBN: 9781999368432
e-book: 9781999368494

www.charcopress.com

Edited by Fionn Petch
Cover designed by Pablo Font
Typeset by Laura Jones
Proofread by Fiona Mackintosh

8   10   9

Supported using public funding by
ARTS COUNCIL
ENGLAND

LOTTERY FUNDED

Shortlisted
INTERNATIONAL BOOKER PRIZE 2022

Winner of
DASHIELL HAMMETT PRIZE 2021
For *Catedrales* [Cathedrals]

Winner of
VALENCIA NEGRA PRIZE 2021
For *Catedrales* [Cathedrals]

Winner of
**NEGRA Y CRIMINAL PRIZE
TENERIFE NOIR 2021**
For her body of work

Winner of
**PEPE CARVALHO CRIME FICTION PRIZE
(Spain) 2019**
For her lifetime achievements

Winner of
**BLUE METROPOLIS PRIZE
(Canada) 2019**
For her body of work

Winner of
**NATIONAL PRIZE FOR NOVELS
(Argentina) 2018**
For *Un comunista en calzoncillos*
[A Communist in Underpants]

Winner of
**XII ROSALÍA DE CASTRO PRIZE
(Spain) 2014**
For her literary career

Claudia Piñeiro

ELENA KNOWS

Translated by
Frances Riddle

CHARCO PRESS

To my mother

Now he understood her, who had lived beside him so many years and been loved but never understood. You were never truly together with one you loved until the person in question was dead and actually inside you.

Thomas Bernhard, *Gargoyles*
(trans. Richard and Clara Winston)

Even a concrete building is nothing but a house of cards. It's just waiting for the right gust of wind.

Thomas Bernhard,
The Forest is Large, and So is the Darkness
(trans. Douglas Robertson)

I

MORNING

(SECOND PILL)

1

The trick is to lift up the right foot, just a few centimetres off the floor, move it forward through the air, just enough to get past the left foot, and when it gets as far as it can go, lower it. That's all it is, Elena thinks. But she thinks this, and even though her brain orders the movement, her right foot doesn't move. It does not lift up. It does not move forward through the air. It does not lower back down. It's so simple. But it doesn't do it. So Elena sits and waits. In her kitchen. She has to take the train into the city at ten o'clock; the one after that, the eleven o'clock, won't do because she took the pill at nine, so she thinks, and she knows, that she has to take the ten o'clock train, right after the medication has managed to persuade her body to follow her brain's orders. Soon. The eleven o'clock train won't do because by then the medicine's effect will have diminished and almost disappeared and she'll be back to where she is now, but without any hope that the levodopa will take effect. Levodopa is the name for the chemical that will begin circulating in her body once the pill has dissolved; she has known that name for a while now. Levodopa. The doctor said it and she wrote it down for herself on a piece of paper because she knew she wasn't going to understand the doctor's handwriting. She knows that the levodopa is moving through her body. All she can do now is wait. She counts the streets. She recites the names from memory. From first to last and last to first. Lupo, Moreno, 25 de Mayo, Mitre, Roca. Roca, Mitre, 25 de Mayo, Moreno, Lupo. Levodopa. It's only five blocks to the train station, it's not that many, she thinks, and she continues reciting the street names, and continues waiting. Five. She can't yet shuffle down those five blocks but she can silently repeat the street names. She hopes she doesn't run into anyone she knows today. No one who will ask after her health or give her their belated condolences over the death of her daughter. Every day there's some new person who couldn't make it to the vigil or the burial. Or who didn't dare to. Or didn't want to. When someone like Rita dies, everyone feels invited to the funeral. That's why ten o'clock is the worst time, she thinks, because to get to the station she has to pass by the bank and today's the day the pensions are paid, so it's very likely that she'll run into some neighbour or other. Or several. Even though the bank doesn't open until ten, just as her train should be arriving at the station and she'll be there ready to board, ticket in hand, before that, Elena knows, she's going to have to pass the pensioners lined up outside as if they're afraid the money will run out so they have to get there early. She can avoid going past the bank if she walks round the block, but that's something the Parkinson's won't allow. That's its name. Elena knows she hasn't been the one in charge of some parts of her body for a while now, her feet, for example. He's in charge. Or she. And she wonders if Parkinson's is masculine or feminine, because even though the name sounds masculine it's still an illness, and an illness is something feminine. Just like a misfortune. Or a curse. And so she thinks she should address it as Herself, because when she thinks about it, she thinks 'fucking whore illness.' And a whore is a she, not a he. If Herself will excuse my language. Dr Benegas explained it to her several times but she still doesn't understand; she understands what she has because it's inside her body, but not some of the words that the doctor uses. Rita was there when he first explained the disease. Rita, who's now dead. He told them that Parkinson's was a degradation of the cells of the nervous system. And both she and her daughter disliked that word. Degradation. And Dr Benegas must've noticed, because he quickly tried to explain. And he said, an illness of the central nervous system that degrades, or mutates, or changes, or modifies the nerve cells in such a way that they stop producing dopamine. And then Elena learned that when her brain orders her feet to move, for example, the order only reaches her feet if the dopamine takes it there. Like a messenger, she thought that day. So Parkinson's is Herself and dopamine is the messenger. And her brain is nothing, she thinks, because her feet don't listen to it. Like a dethroned king who doesn't realise he's not in charge anymore. Like the emperor with no clothes from the story she used to tell Rita when she was little. The dethroned king, the emperor with no clothes. And now there's Herself, not Elena but her illness, the messenger, and the dethroned king. Elena repeats the names like she repeated the streets she has to pass to get to the station; the names keep her company while she waits. From first to last and last to first. She doesn't like the emperor with no clothes because it means he's naked. She prefers the dethroned king. She waits, she repeats, she breaks them into pairs: Herself and the messenger; the messenger and the king, the king and Herself. She tries again but her feet are still foreign to her, not merely disobedient, but deaf. Deaf feet. Elena would love to shout at them,

3

Move, feet, hurry up! Dammit, she'd even shout, *Move and hurry up, dammit,* but she knows it would be useless, because her feet won't listen to her voice either. So she doesn't shout, she waits. She silently recites the streets, kings, streets again. She adds new words to her prayer: dopamine, levodopa. She makes the connection between the dopa of dopamine and of levodopa, they must be related, but she's just guessing, she doesn't know for sure, she recites the words, plays with them, she lets her tongue get twisted, she waits, and she doesn't care, she only cares that the time passes, that the pill dissolves, that it moves through her body to her feet so that they will finally get the message that they have to start moving.

She's nervous, which isn't good, because when she gets nervous the medication takes longer to work. But she can't help it. Today's the day she's going to play her last card, to try to find out who killed her daughter, to talk to the only person in the world who she thinks she can convince to help her. Because of a long-ago debt, something almost forgotten. She's going to call in that debt, though if Rita were here she wouldn't approve, *life's not a swap meet, Mum, some things are done because God wills it.* It's not going to be easy, but she's going to try. Isabel is the name of the woman she's looking for. She's not sure if Isabel will remember her. Probably not. She'll remember Rita, though, she sends her a Christmas card every year. She might not know about Rita's death. If no one told her, if she didn't read the obituary that the Catholic school where Rita worked finally ran two days after the burial, saying that the administration, staff and student body are united in grief at her sudden loss. If she doesn't find Isabel today, she will almost certainly send another card this December, addressed to a dead woman, wishing her a merry Christmas and a happy New Year. She definitely remembers Rita, but her, Elena, probably not. And even if she remembers her she won't recognise her, trapped, hunched, inside a deteriorating body that doesn't match her age. It will be Elena's job to explain who she is and why she's there, when she confronts Isabel. She's going to tell her about Rita. And about her death. Or rather she'll tell her the little she understands from everything they've told her. Elena knows where to find Isabel, but not how to get there, even though she went there herself, twenty years ago, alongside Rita. If luck is on her side, if Isabel hasn't moved, or if she hasn't died like her daughter died, she'll find her there, in that old house in Belgrano that has a heavy wooden door with bronze fittings, right beside some doctors' offices. She doesn't remember the name of the street, if she could just recall the question that her daughter asked her that day, *Have you ever heard of a street called Soldado de la Independencia, Mum?* then she would know. She'll know soon, because she remembers that it's one or two blocks from the avenue that runs along the edge of Buenos Aires from Retiro Station to the General Paz Highway, near a little plaza beside the train tracks. They didn't see the train, but they heard it pass by and Rita asked which line it was. But Isabel didn't answer, because she was crying too hard. To find out how to get there, this second time, almost twenty years later, Elena went to the private car service which had opened a few years back on the corner of her street, replacing the bakery where Elena had bought bread every day since moving to the neighbourhood as a new bride, until one day the bread disappeared and the cars showed up. The driver didn't know, *I'm new*, he apologised and he asked the owner. He repeated Elena's words, *The avenue that runs along the edge of Buenos Aires, from Retiro to the General Paz, near the train tracks.* And the owner answered, *Libertador.* And Elena said *Yes, that's it, Libertador*, as soon as they said it she remembered, and she told them that she had to go to Belgrano, to a little plaza. *Olleros*, said another driver who had just returned from a trip. *I don't know the name*, said Elena. *Olleros*, repeated the man, confidently, but she didn't remember the name of the street, just the wooden door, and the bronze fittings, and Isabel, and her husband, very little about her husband. *Shall we take you?* the owner asked her and Elena said no, that it was a long trip, a big expense, that she was going to go by train and if necessary, if she couldn't make it on her own and her body didn't feel up for the subway, she'd take a taxi near Constitución. *We can give you a good deal,* the owner offered. *No, thank you,* she answered. *You can pay later,* he insisted. *I'll take the train,* said Elena, *I don't like debts.* They weren't going to change her mind. *There's no subway near there, ma'am. The closest station is Carranza, but from there you'd have to walk like ten blocks*, one of the drivers said. *If you go by taxi be careful not to let them take you for a ride, tell the driver to go straight down 9 de Julio to Libertador and from there straight on to Olleros. Well, no*, the driver who knew the way corrected him, *because Libertador turns into Figueroa Alcorta, before the Planetarium they'll have to be careful to turn to the left, towards the Spanish Monument, and then retake Libertador there. Or at the Palermo Hippodrome*, the owner added, *but don't let them take you for a ride, are you sure you don't want us to drive you?* Elena left without answering, because she'd already answered that question and it was enough of an effort for her already without having to answer everything twice.

Constitución, 9 de Julio, Libertador, Figueroa Alcorta, Planetarium, Spanish Monument, Libertador, Olleros, a wooden door, bronze fittings, a door, Olleros, Libertador, 9 de Julio, Constitución. Last to first and first to last. She doesn't know at what point in the prayer she should add the Hippodrome. She waits, she thinks, she counts the streets again. Five blocks to the station, and then so many more she doesn't know, or she doesn't remember, to call in a debt because she has no other choice. King without a crown. Herself. From her position, seated, she tries to lift her right foot in the air, the foot now responds to the message and rises. So she's ready, she knows. She places her palms on her seated thighs, she puts her two feet together so that her knees are at ninety-degree angles, then she crosses her right hand to her left shoulder and her left hand on her right shoulder, she begins to rock back and forth on the chair and then, with the momentum, she stands up. That's how Dr Benegas has taught her to stand up, and she knows it's harder that way but she tries it as often as she can, she practises, because she wants to be able to do it at her next check-up. She wants to impress Dr Benegas, show him that she can do it, despite the things he told her during their last appointment, two weeks before Rita was found dead. Standing in front of the chair she raises her right foot, she holds it up in the air, just a few centimetres, she moves it forward until it gets far enough past the left foot so that the movement can be called a step, then she lowers it, and now it's the left foot's turn to do the same thing, exactly the same thing. Move up and through the air. Lower down. Up, over, down.

That's all it is. Nothing more than that. Just walking, to get to the ten o'clock train.

2

Rita died on a rainy afternoon. On a shelf in her room there was a glass sea lion that turned purplish pink when the humidity in the air neared one hundred percent and precipitation was imminent. That was the colour it had the day she died. She'd bought it one summer in Mar del Plata. Elena and Rita had gone on holiday as they'd always done, every two years, up until Elena's illness began to make a mockery of her shameful attempts at motion. The years they didn't travel they stayed home and used their savings to paint the house or do repairs that couldn't be put off any longer, like fixing a broken pipe, changing a worn-out mattress, having a new sewage pit dug. The last year they'd stayed home they'd had to replace almost all the back patio tiles because the roots of a paraíso tree, which wasn't even theirs, had surreptitiously crept under their yard from the other side of the fence. The years that they went on holiday it was always to the coast, to Mar del Plata. They rented a two-room house off Colón Avenue, one block before it begins to climb the hill that later slopes down to the sea. Rita slept in the bedroom and Elena in the living-dining area. *You get up so early, Mum, it's better for you to be near the kitchen so you don't bother me.* Just like they did every two years, Rita had circled the classified ads for apartments within their budget, to later choose based on the one whose owner lived closest to their house, so they wouldn't have to go too far to pay and pick up the key, and in the end all the places were pretty much the same, a few extra plates or a nicer upholstery weren't going to affect their holiday. They would go together to close the deal. Even though they would take the apartment regardless, they'd ask to see pictures and the owners would show them photos that were never a faithful representation of reality, that never showed any grime. But that wasn't a problem either, because Elena liked to clean, back when she still had a body that could do so. Scrubbing relaxed her and even miraculously eased her back pain. In just one afternoon the apartment was what it was, but it was clean. They didn't go to the beach. Too many people, too hot. Rita didn't like to carry the umbrella, and Elena refused to set foot on the sand if she didn't have guaranteed shade. But it was a change of scenery, and that was good. They slept a bit more, they ate fresh-baked croissants for breakfast, they cooked lots of fresh fish, and every afternoon, when the sun began to tuck itself behind the apartment buildings, they went out to walk the Rambla. They walked from south to north along the seafront and returned north to south along the avenue. They argued. Always, every afternoon. About anything. The topic was unimportant, what mattered was their chosen mode of communicating. Arguments layered on top of each other, one hidden beneath another, lying in wait and ready to leap forth, no matter how unrelated to the topic at hand. They fought as if each word thrown out were the crack of a whip, leather in motion, one of them lashed out, then the other. Blistering the rival's body with words. Neither let on that she was hurt. They stopped just short of an actual physical altercation but went on until one of the two, usually Rita, sped up to walk several steps ahead, muttering angrily under her breath, abandoning the fight more out of fear of her own words than any pain felt or provoked.

She spotted the glass sea lion on the first day of their holiday one year, in a store that sold conch necklaces, ashtrays shaped like the Torreón del Monje, jewellery boxes decorated with tiny shells, corkscrews in the form of the anatomy of a little boy, a priest, or a gaucho, which neither of them dared to look at, and other souvenirs of that nature. Rita stopped in front of the window and tapped the glass with the recently-filed nail of her index finger and said, *Before we leave I'm going to buy that.* Weather-Predicting Seal: Blue=Sunny, Pink=Rain, said the sign stuck to the glass, written in bright blue capital letters. Elena didn't approve, *Don't waste your money on stupid trinkets; it's hard enough for you to make it in the first place. I'm going to spend it on what I please. Your sense of pleasure is impaired. Let's not talk about impairments. You're right, we have your friend at the bank for that. At least I have a man that loves me. If that makes you happy, dear. It's hard to be happy anywhere near you, Mum,* Rita dealt her final blow and took several long strides to move ahead. From the rear, Elena followed in her daughter's wake while maintaining the established distance, then just a few paces later she cracked her own whip, *With that rotten personality you'll never be happy. What's inherited can't be stolen, Mum, Is that so,* Elena responded, and they fell silent. When they got to the Hotel Provincial they turned around and headed back south. They repeated the same routine every day. The walk, the whip cracks, the distance, and finally the silence. The words changed, the reasons behind the fights were different, but the cadence, the tone, the routine, never varied, They didn't mention the sea lion again, although one afternoon when they passed the souvenir and seashell store Elena laughed and said, *Why don't you take the priest corkscrew to Father Juan?* but her daughter didn't think it was funny, *You're so filthy-minded, Mum.*

Before the two weeks were up, just as Rita had declared, she bought the weather-predicting seal. She paid for it in cash. She had a debit card she'd received when the school officially hired her and set up direct deposit payments into her account, but she never carried the card with her out of fear it might get stolen. She asked them to wrap the seal in a lot of paper so it wouldn't break but they used bubble wrap instead and Rita enjoyed popping it later, after she'd ridden with the sea lion on her lap the whole bus ride home.

Elena still keeps it, like she keeps all of Rita's things. She put everything in a big cardboard box that her neighbour's twenty-nine-inch TV had come in. The neighbour had taken it out with the trash and Elena asked him if she could have it. To put away Rita's things, she told him, and he gave it to her without saying a word, but like he was silently giving his condolences. He even helped her take it into her house. Elena put everything inside it. Everything except the clothes; she couldn't stand to put the clothes in, they still had her smell, the smell of her daughter. Clothes always retain a person's smell, Elena knows, even if they're washed a thousand times with different detergents. It's not the smell of the perfume or deodorant the person wore or the laundry soap it was washed with when there was still someone to stain it. It's not the smell of the house or the family because Elena's clothes don't have the same smell. It's the smell of the dead person when they were alive. The smell of Rita. She couldn't bear to smell that smell and not see her daughter. The same thing happened with her husband's clothes but at the time she had no idea how much more that smell could hurt when it was your child's. So not the clothes. She also didn't want to give them to the church and then have to see Rita's green sweater someday turning the corner keeping somebody else warm. So she burned her daughter's clothes in a pile in the back yard. It took four matches to light it. The first things to catch fire were the nylon stockings, melted by the heat into synthetic lava, then little by little everything began to blaze. There were underwires, snaps, zips left in the ashes afterwards which Elena put in a rubbish bag and took out for the garbage man. So the clothes didn't go into the neighbour's box. But she did put in the shoes, a brand new pair of wool gloves that didn't smell like anything, old photos, Rita's address book, all her important papers except her ID, which she'd had to give to the funeral company so they could take care of the burial, Rita's calendar, her bank cards, her half-finished knitting, the newspaper photo taken of all the teachers the day they inaugurated the new high school, the bible Father Juan had given her, with the inscription *May the word of God accompany you as it did your father*, Rita's reading glasses, her thyroid medication, a little Saint Expeditus prayer card that the school secretary had given her when Elena's retirement pension had taken a long time to go through, the clipping from the newspaper the day Isabel's daughter was born. *Isabel and Marcos Mansilla joyfully announce the birth of their daughter, María Julieta, in the City of Buenos Aires, March 20, 1982.* The announcement was carefully clipped, the edges perfectly straight. The folder with the cards that the Mansillas sent every Christmas. The empty heart-shaped box of chocolates that her friend from the bank had given her which she'd used to keep pieces of paper and a bundle of badly folded letters tied with a pink ribbon. Elena hadn't dared to read the notes, not out of respect for her daughter's privacy, but for her own sake, to avoid learning the details of a story she'd never wanted to know anything about. For some mothers reading their daughter's love letters could be interesting, illicitly thrilling, Elena thinks, affirming that the daughter had become a woman, that she was desired, that she was on her way to fulfilling her duty to the species, following the cycle of birth, maturity, reproduction, and death, knowing her torch would continue on in the world. Elena looks at the bundle of cards and she thinks about that word, torch. Torch. This wasn't the case with Rita, she wasn't a young woman meeting her intended and Roberto Almada was incapable of rising to the circumstances. They were two hopeless creatures, two losers in love, or not even, two lonely people who had never even entered the game, who had contented themselves with watching from the stands. As far as Elena was concerned, it would've been more dignified at that point for her daughter to abstain from playing altogether. But Rita did enter the game, however late, at the age Elena had already been widowed. She suspects little happened between them, just a few kisses and some clumsy groping in the plaza as the sun disappeared behind the monument to the nation's flag, or at Roberto's house before his mother got home from the beauty salon. Whatever happened, she prefers not to know, much less to read about it in those letters, more terrified of the words Roberto wrote in response to her daughter than of what they might've done. So she did not untie the ribbon, she did not let the bow come undone to expose those papers full of words, she hardly touched them as she put them back in the box of chocolates and dropped it into the big box that the neighbour gave her, along with all of the other belongings left over after the fire took everything that smelled like her daughter.

Everything except the little sea lion. She placed the weather-predicting seal on a shelf in the dining room, between the radio and the telephone, but pushed a few centimetres forward. A distance proportional to the one Rita and Elena maintained after each fight. A prime location. So she could see it every day, so she'd never forget that, on the afternoon Rita died, it was raining.

3

Elena advances towards the station. Five blocks lie ahead of her. First things first. She'll walk five blocks, she'll look out of the corner of her eye at the open window of the ticket booth, she'll say round trip to Plaza Constitución, open her coin purse, remove the coins that she counted out last night for the exact cost of the ticket, stretch out her hand, let the ticket seller take the coins and give her the ticket, grip the little piece of paper that allows her to travel, not letting it fall, put it in the pocket of her cardigan, and once she's sure she won't lose it, descend the stairs holding on to the rail, if possible on the right side because that's the arm that responds best to what the brain orders, at the bottom of the stairs turn left, walk through the tunnel, trying not to breathe in the smell of urine that saturates the walls, the ceiling, and the floor which Elena drags her feet across, the same acrid smell since the day she crossed the tunnel for the first time long before she ever needed any pill to help her walk, when she still knew nothing about dethroned kings or messengers, holding Rita's hand when she was a little girl or several steps behind her when she stopped being little, always the same smell of urine that burns her nostrils just thinking about it, always with her mouth closed and lips pressed tight to avoid inhaling it, and never opening her mouth a crack, dodging the woman selling garlic and spices, the boy who sells pirated CDs that she wouldn't be able to play, the girl who sells key rings with coloured lights and alarm clocks that sound as she walks by, or the man with no legs who holds out his hand for coins like she held hers out a few minutes ago for the train ticket, turn again to the left, go up the same number of steps that she just went down and then, finally, step onto the platform. But all that, Elena knows, will be after she's managed to walk those five blocks she still hasn't walked. She's just finished the first one. Someone says hello. Her stiff neck forces her to walk looking down at the ground so she doesn't see who it is. Sternocleidomastoid is the name of the muscle that restricts her movement. The one that pulls her head down. Sternocleidomastoid, Dr Benegas had said, and Elena asked him to write it down, *In capital letters, Doctor, or I won't understand your handwriting*, so that she wouldn't forget, so that even if her executioner wore a hood, she would know his name and be able to include him in the prayer she recites while she waits. The person who greeted her continues on their way and although she glances out of the corner of her eye she doesn't recognise the back moving away in the opposite direction, but she says good morning anyway, because the person who greeted her said *Good morning, Elena*, and if they know her name they warrant a greeting. At the first corner she waits for a car to pass and then she crosses the street. With her head down, all she can see are the worn tyres as they approach, pass her, and then move away. She steps off the pavement, walks quickly taking short steps, scraping along the hot asphalt, steps onto the pavement of the next block, pauses for a second, just a second, and continues on. A few steps ahead the black and white checkerboard paving tiles let her know she's walking past the midwife's house. Rita refused to set foot on those tiles ever since the day she learned that abortions were performed inside that house. *She's an abortionist, not a midwife, Mum. Who told you that? Father Juan. And how does he know? Because he gives confession to everyone in the neighbourhood, Mum, of course he knows. And doesn't he have to keep what he hears in confession confidential? He didn't tell me who had the abortion, Mum, just where. And that isn't covered by the confidentiality of confession? No. Who told you it isn't? Father Juan.* Elena, to humour Rita, didn't walk past the house either, they always crossed the street and walked on the other pavement and then crossed back over once they'd passed it, as if they were afraid stepping on those tiles would somehow contaminate them, or make them complicit, as if just walking past the house were some sin. But Rita isn't here, someone killed her, Elena knows, even though everyone else says something different, and while she'd like to respect her dead daughter's memory she can't allow herself the luxury of observing all her rituals. On that very checkerboard pavement is where Rita met Isabel, the woman she's going to try to find, she makes the connection for the first time, and then she steps more confidently, calmly, as if the checkerboard her daughter had cursed so many times suddenly made sense. She hesitates when she reaches the end of the second block. If she goes straight it's only three blocks to the ticket booth where she'll say round trip to Plaza Constitución, but that route will take her past the bank where the pensioners are waiting in line, and it's quite likely she'll run into someone she knows, that that someone will want to give her their condolences, that they will hold her up longer than she wants them to, and then she'll miss the ten o'clock train. If she goes round the block she'll have to add three more blocks to her route, and that would be asking too much of her illness. Elena doesn't like owing Herself any favours. No debts and no favours. Herself would make her regret it, Elena knows, because she knows Herself almost as well as she knew her daughter. Fucking whore illness. Before, when she had just a little difficulty getting her left arm into the sleeve of her coat, when she'd still never heard of Madopar or levodopa and her shuffling gait didn't yet have a name, before her neck began to force her to always stare at her shoes, she would avoid going past the bank. Even though back then there was no risk of condolences, she did it anyway, to avoid running into Roberto Almada, Rita's friend, the son of the hairdresser. *My boyfriend, Mum. A person of your age can't have a boyfriend. What do you want me to call him then? Roberto, that's more than enough.* But she isn't up to taking the longer route now. When the pavement switches to grey tiles, larger and glossier than any others on her route, Elena knows she's walking past the bank. *They're special tiles designed for heavy foot traffic, Elena, made locally but just as good as the Italian ones,* Roberto had explained proudly when talking about the place he'd worked since age eighteen. Now she can see, out of the corner of her eye, a row of shoes lined up in front of the door. She can see the wearers of the shoes up to the knee. She doesn't see any trainers or jeans. Just worn loafers, espadrilles, a sandal covering a bandaged foot and ankle. Purple feet, crisscrossed by veins, freckly, spotted, swollen. All old feet, she thinks, the feet of the old people who are worried the money will run out. She doesn't look at them, she's afraid she'll recognise a leg and she prefers not to stop. Then, once the line has ended and she feels safe, once there's no longer a row of shoes to her left, someone says *Good morning, Elena*, but she keeps going as if she hasn't heard. But then the person speeds up, touches her shoulder. Roberto Almada, the man Rita insisted on calling her boyfriend. The cripple, as Elena called him in front of her daughter to provoke her. Or the hunchback, as the neighbourhood kids called him when he was a boy. Elena can't see his hump, she can just barely raise her eyes to the height of his chest with great effort, but she knows Roberto's back begins to curve around at the shoulder blades. *Hello, Doña Elena*, he says again, and his formal tone hits Elena between the eyes. *Oh, Roberto, I didn't recognise you, you got new shoes, didn't you?* He looks at his shoes and says *Yes, they're new*. They both go silent, Elena's worn out shoes beside Roberto's shiny new ones. Roberto shifts his feet uncomfortably, *Mum wanted to send her love and says you should stop by the hair salon sometime, if you liked your last haircut she'll give you another one, on the house*. Elena thanks him, even though she knows that the last time, the only time she went to Roberto's mother's beauty salon was the afternoon that her daughter died, but she stops her thoughts before they can go too far in that direction, because she can't afford the luxury. If she lets her mind wander back to that afternoon she'll miss her train, so she wills herself to shoo them away and remain focused on the present, on Roberto. What she'd like to have done at his mother's beauty parlour is to have the shadow of fuzz removed from her face again, and to have her toenails cut. She clips her fingernails herself, or she files them, but she can't do her feet. She hasn't been able to reach them for a while now and since Rita's death the nail of her big toe has begun to scratch the tip of her shoe and she's afraid that it might break off in a bad spot, or worse, rip open the worn leather of her shoe. Rita cut them for her every two weeks, she brought a washbowl with warm water, a piece of white soap inside to soften her calluses, and a clean towel, always the same one, that she washed after every time and put away with the washbowl. She scrunched up her face in disgust as she cut her mother's toenails, dirty, flaky and yellowed, swollen from the water like a dry sponge. But she did it, putting Elena's foot on her knee as she worked. And when she was done she washed her hands with dish soap, one, two, three times, then, with the excuse of disinfecting the towel from any possible fungus, she washed her hands with bleach. *What do people who don't have daughters to cut their toenails do, Rita? They let them get long and filthy, Mum.*

I deposited your cheque for you like I said I would, Roberto says. And Elena thanks him again and she forgets about her nails. After Rita's death, Roberto had offered to take care of depositing her pension, *So you don't have to wait in line, what with your health. What health, Roberto?* Elena had asked. *So you don't have to trouble yourself. And since when do you care about my troubles? I always cared about you, Elena, and your illness, don't be unfair. Go to hell, Roberto,* she'd said, but she'd accepted his help. Before, Rita had taken care of going to the bank, but now she was gone, and even though Elena didn't like the man, having a friend inside the bank had its advantages. *If you only knew how much I miss your daughter,* she hears him say, and Elena hates his words as much as she imagines she'd hate the words written on the letters she didn't read, the ones she keeps in the box her neighbour gave her, tied up with a special ribbon that Rita picked out for them. She knows he couldn't have killed her, not because of what he says, not because of what he was doing that day, not because he'd be incapable of murder, but because a cripple like him would've been no match for Rita. Very few people would've been a match for Rita, and even so the truth eludes her, it's hard for her to imagine who it could've been, that's why she needs help, because no one has been accused, there aren't even any suspects, or motives, or theories, just the death. *I'm in a hurry here, I don't want to miss the ten o'clock train*, Elena says and starts to raise her foot in the air so she can continue walking when he asks, *You're going to travel alone? I live alone, Roberto*, she says without pausing the step she's already begun. After a brief silence he says, *On you go then, on you go.* And she's already going, towards the station. She glances down at the pavement and she knows that Roberto is still behind her, because his shoes are still there, two stains of black leather that gleam almost as bright as the paving tiles they stand on, pointing in the direction she's walking, alone, without anyone to accompany her, with the nail of her big toe stabbing into her shoe as she follows the route that will take her, after two more blocks, to the ticket booth where she'll get the ticket that she'll grip tightly in her clenched fist until it's safely stowed in the pocket of her cardigan, then she'll go down the stairs, through the urine-soaked tunnel, and up to the platform to wait, tired, bent over, for the ten o'clock train.

4

Rita was found hanging from the church belfry. Dead. On a rainy afternoon. That, the rain, Elena knows, is an important detail. Even though everyone says it was suicide. Friend or not, everyone says so. But as much as they try to convince her, or remain silent, no one can refute the fact that Rita never went near the church when it even threatened rain. She wouldn't be caught dead there, her mother would've said if anyone had asked her before. But she can't say that now, because there she was, that lifeless body that was no longer her daughter, hanging from the belfry one rainy day, although no one could explain how she'd got there. Rita had been afraid of lightning, ever since she was a little girl, and she knew that the cross on top of the church attracted it. *It's the town lightning rod*, her father had taught her without knowing that this passing comment would keep her from going anywhere near the place in stormy weather. If rain was forecast she kept away from the church and from the Inchauspes' house too, the only one in the neighbourhood with a pool at that time. Water is an excellent conductor of electricity and pools are magnets for lightning, she'd heard an engineer say on a news report about an accident at a country club when two kids ignored the No Swimming sign during a storm and were killed by a bolt of lightning. And if over the years more pools were built in the neighbourhood, or more lightning rods, she preferred not to know, because every new titbit of information would only further limit her movements. Not stepping on the checkerboard tiles outside the midwife's, not going to church on rainy days, and not going near the Inchauspes' house complicated things enough without adding any other detours. Not to mention that Rita patted her right buttock whenever she passed a redhead, as she recited with the solemn tone of the Hail Mary: Ginger, ginger, you're no danger. Ginger, ginger, I give you the finger. Ginger, ginger, who's the sinner?, or she touched her right hand to her left breast if anyone mentioned Liberti, a poor old man who was rumoured around the neighbourhood to be cursed because he was always at the wrong place at the wrong time: in front of the Ferraris' house when the pine tree fell and smashed the roof, queuing at the bank when the widow Gande's pension was stolen from her, standing on the corner when Dr Benegas hit the bin lorry with his brand new car, and other incidents of the kind. It's better not to know, said Rita. When she started working at the Catholic school, at age seventeen, a few weeks after her dad's death and because Father Juan appealed to the board to give the position to the dead man's daughter, despite her age, Rita learned to make up excuses every time they tried to send her to the chapel in inclement weather. Pressing tasks, stomach pains, a headache, she'd go as far as to fake a fainting fit. Whatever it took to avoid going near that cross on a rainy day. That's how she'd always been.

And Elena thinks, she knows, that this couldn't have just changed all of a sudden, even on the day of her death.

Even though no one will listen to her, even though no one cares. If her daughter went to the church on a rainy day it was because someone dragged her there, dead or alive. *Someone or something*, said Inspector Avellaneda, the officer assigned to the case. *Why do you say that, Inspector, something like what? Oh, I don't know*, said Avellaneda. *If you don't know, then don't say anything*, she scolded him.

She was found by some boys that Father Juan had assigned to ring the bells announcing the seven o'clock mass. They flew back down the stairs screaming and ran through the nave to the sacristy. Father Juan didn't believe them, saying, *Get out of here, you little devils*, but the boys insisted he had to come and see and they dragged him up the belfry. The body was hanging from a rope, and the rope from the same yoke that held the bronze bell. An old rope so worn out no one could explain how it held her weight for long enough to kill her. It had been left lying in the belfry along with some scaffolding boards from the last time they cleaned the dome, according to the report Elena later read. *My God*, murmured Father Juan and although he recognised her immediately he didn't say her name, pretended he didn't know her, just picked up the overturned chair beneath the swinging body and stood on it to take her pulse. *She's dead*, he said, which the boys already knew because they'd played at being dead many times, being cops or robbers, shooting to kill or dying, so they knew that the woman hanging from the bell was not playing. Father Juan took them back to the sacristy, but this time he had them make the sign of the cross and bend their knees slightly when they passed the sanctum holding the communion wafers that had already been blessed. *You wait here*, he said to them, and he phoned the police. He asked the inspector to wait until after the seven o'clock mass since people were already coming into the church and he didn't want to cancel the service, especially since it was the Thursday after Pentecost, the Solemnity of Corpus Christi, the Day of the Most Holy Body and Blood of Jesus Christ the Lord. *And anyway there's nothing more we can do for the woman now, except pray, Inspector.* The inspector agreed it was best not to interrupt the service, *A dead man is a dead man, Father, or rather a dead woman, and it's going to be a heavy blow for the people, terrible, it's better they go in peace and find out tomorrow, what about the family, do you know the woman, Father? She doesn't have a family, Inspector, just the mother, who's sick, I don't know how she's going to take it. Don't worry, Father, we'll handle it, to Caesar what is of Caesar and to God what is of God.* The inspector hung up and started to get things ready, it would take time to recall the car, which was out on patrol, gather a few officers, and notify the coroner. *You two wait here and don't move, don't even think about going back up there*, Father Juan told the boys as he put on his robe for mass, *And not a word to anyone, God will be watching you*, he added, but it wasn't necessary, because they'd both gone mute, sunk down in the sacristy couch.

No bells announced mass that evening, but there was a mass. If anyone had paid attention and also had a good memory, they would remember that in the silence of the church all that could be heard was the sound of the rain falling in the courtyard. But no one paid any attention to the rain that evening except Elena. A memory for details, Elena knows, is only for the brave, and being cowardly or brave is not something one can choose.

The Father said, *In the name of the Father*, and everyone stood and made the sign of the cross with their backs to the body swinging from the bell yoke not so many metres above them, oblivious. There were some twenty people there, with their wet umbrellas lying across the many empty pews. From the altar Father Juan could see the balcony where the organ stood and where the choir sang on Sundays. Beside the organ he could see the first steps of the stairway leading to the belfry. He'd never realised that they were visible from the altar. *He should have fed them also with the finest of the wheat: and with honey out of the rock should I have satisfied thee, hallelujah.* Before the Creed the first police officer entered the church. The squeal of the hinges on the wooden door made several people turn around to see who was coming in at that hour, so late that the mass wouldn't even count. It was strange to see a police officer at the seven o'clock mass and even stranger to see one in uniform, but the officer quickly took off his wet hat, made the sign of the cross and sat in the last row as if he'd come to hear the word of God. *Brothers: I learned from the Lord what I have taught you, and it is this: that the Lord Jesus Christ, on the night he was betrayed took bread, and giving thanks, he said the blessing, broke the bread and gave it to his disciples.* After communion two more officers arrived but taking off their wet hats and making the sign of the cross wasn't enough to banish suspicions this time, even though they tried to hide their standard-issue firearms behind their hats. A murmur grew among the parishioners. Several women snatched up their purses from the pew and hung them on their arms, either out of fear that the police were after some thief inside the church and that the thief in his escape attempt might try to take their purse; or afraid that some imminent yet still unknown event might require them to take off running at a moment's notice; or just because they saw the other women do so. *Each one must examine himself before he eats of the bread and drinks of the cup. For he that eateth and drinketh unworthily, eateth and drinketh damnation to himself.* As the people who were able to take communion, or who weren't but did so anyway, were walking back down the aisles with the wafer stuck to the roofs of their mouths, the sound was heard, at first it was an ambiguous creak, hard to attribute to a precise origin, and then a thud, that echoed. All heads turned and looked up, except for Father Juan, who just raised his eyes. The three officers put on their hats and stood. *In you they hope, Lord, and on you are fixed the eyes of everyone, he that eateth my flesh and drinketh of my blood dwelleth in me and I in him*. From the altar, as he put away the wafers that hadn't been handed out at communion, Father Juan watched the three officers rush up the stairs that led to the belfry and disappear. The people watched too, and then looked at Father Juan as if demanding an explanation. *Receive the bad, the good: for this full life, for that mortal feast*. The rope had finally snapped, the weight of the body undid the knot and Rita, dead, fell onto the floor of the belfry. *Both the wicked and the good eat of this celestial food: but with ends how opposite!* The priest stood up, and walked to the centre of the altar to give the final blessing. *You who live and reign, forever and ever.* And they could go in peace. *I ask you all to please leave and go to your homes, there is nothing you can do here, not for yourselves or for anyone else.* He herded his flock to the door, and at the insistence of some he had to explain, *Someone hanged themselves in the belfry*, but he didn't say who, and once everyone had left Father Juan went up the tower of his church. In addition to the three officers there was a man in a suit, someone who had gone up without the priest seeing him. *Who are you? That's the coroner*, one of the officers answered. The coroner took notes, an officer drew a chalk outline of Rita's body on the concrete floor, another took photos, and the third carefully wound up the rope that had been around her neck and put it in a plastic bag. On a white label, as the coroner and the priest watched, he wrote: Evidence #1. One of the few pieces of evidence they would find.

5

Sitting on a bench at the station, she waits. It is made of concrete and the cold seeps through her skirt. Someone heats water inside the hotdog stand. There aren't too many people around, more than she would prefer but not so many that she won't find a seat once the train pulls into the station and she gets on it. The earlier trains, the seven o'clock, the eight o'clock and even the nine o'clock, Elena knows, would've been impossible, too many people waiting, too many people squeezing in through the same doors, too many passengers inside the train. But for people who have to arrive at work on time, who wake up early every morning to get to the office, a school, a bank, the ten o'clock train is no good. The ten o'clock train isn't even any good for people who work in shops, because they wouldn't get to Constitución until almost eleven o'clock, and by that hour the city is already exhausted from so much coming and going. There aren't many people who can start their days late enough to share the ten o'clock train with Elena, just the few who don't belong to that universe of people forced to get up early. A group of teenagers on the cusp of adulthood stand laughing and hugging their notebooks, pushing each other every once in a while to emphasise a joke. Two men in suits, one at each end of the platform, both reading the same newspaper, maybe the same line of the same article, without knowing it. A married couple fights about the price of a medication the man has just bought. The next train to Plaza Constitución will arrive at 10:01 on platform number two, a garbled voice blares over the loudspeaker. A woman and her daughter sit on the bench next to Elena. The girl's feet don't reach the ground, Elena watches her swing them in the air. She knows the girl is looking at her. She knows that she leans over to her mother and whispers something in her ear. *I'll tell you later*, the mother says, and the girl swings her legs faster than before. Elena stares forward, never raising her head higher than Herself will allow. Litter has accumulated below the platform opposite them, some of it will disintegrate with time, Elena knows, some of it will outlive her: the plastic bottles, polystyrene cups, the chunks of concrete. Someone walks by whistling. The whistle gradually fades until it is drowned out by a sound like a far-off stampede. Elena's feet shake and she wonders if it's the floor that's making her tremble or Herself, and even though she doesn't know the answer she grabs the edge of the bench almost out of instinct, aware that nothing bad is going to happen, that this platform, this bench, these walls are sick to death of so much repeated trembling without anything happening, without anyone even noticing except Elena. The woman and the girl stand up and move to the end of the platform. The mother takes the girl by the hand, pulling her along, saying *Hurry up*, but the girl stumbles as she walks forward but looks back, at Elena who's trying to stand up from the same bench where she sat swinging her legs. *What's wrong with that old lady, Mum? I'll tell you later*, the mother says again. The string of train carriages whizz past Elena like a gust of wind, the noise of their weight on the tracks, the screech of metal on metal blocking out all other sounds. Until little by little the gust loses speed, the noise quiets and sounds resume, the blurred images settle, the windows take shape, framing the passengers, who Elena will join, once she manages to stand up. The doors open with a whoosh of decompressed air, Elena's feet shuffle hurriedly to get through before they once again close. There's a crowd of people trying to get on, and Elena leans against the back of the person in front of her to take advantage of their inertia. The whistle blows, someone pushes her from behind and she is thankful. Once inside the train she searches for a seat, any seat, the closest one, and begins to move towards it. The train wobbles, gently, rocking her as she walks. As the train gets going and picks up speed the rocking stops. A young man brushes past her, impatient. She sees the legs of a man coming at her from the other direction, *Excuse me*, the man says when he reaches her, and Elena tries to move aside, but the space gained is hardly noticeable, so the man repeats, *Excuse me, ma'am*, and she tries again to get out of his way but she can't move much more than she already has, so the man turns sideways, raises his arms, lifts his backpack and slides past her. Two rows back she can once again see the empty seat she wants to sit in, but before she makes it there a woman sits down. All she can see is her skirt, a red flowered skirt that flutters with the woman's movement and disappears when she sits. Elena has to start over, she lifts her eyes and wrinkles her forehead, trying to raise her defeated head a little higher, desperately scanning the carriage for another empty seat. When she spots one, she engraves the position in her mind and then lowers her head back down to where Herself wants her to keep it, now with the knowledge that there are two spots at the end of the carriage, which she'll have to walk the length of the aisle to reach. She lifts her right foot and moves it through the air until it passes the left but before lowering it a hand touches hers, *Have a seat here, madam,* says a man whose face she can't see and she says, *Thank you,* and she sits. The man who has just stood up moves to the empty seat at the back of the carriage. Elena clasps her hands in her lap; beside her, in the seat by the window, a man beats his hand against his knee to the rhythm of a music that only he can hear. I hope he's travelling to the last station so he won't ask me to stand up to let him out, Elena thinks, but no sooner has she thought it the man says, *Excuse me, can you let me by?* And without waiting for Elena's answer he stands up in that tiny space between his seat and the back of the seat in front of him waiting for her to move her legs aside, to make enough room for him to pass before the train reaches the next station, *Excuse me,* the man says again and Elena says, *Go ahead, son, go ahead,* but she doesn't move.

6

They took a while to release the body but once the paperwork was complete there was a proper vigil and burial. Everyone came to the funeral. Father Juan, the teachers and other staff of the Catholic school, the neighbours, some of Rita's high school friends she'd kept in touch with and seen from time to time. Roberto Almada and Mimí, his mother, and the girls that worked for her at the hair salon, where they hung a sign on the door, 'Closed for Mourning', over the L'Oréal de Paris logo. Elena chose the casket herself. And the fittings. And the wreath of flowers with golden letters that said 'Your Mother'. *There's no one else in the family that can help you with this?* the funeral parlour director had asked. *There is no family*, she answered. She cried almost unconsciously as she spoke. Elena had never been one for weeping but ever since her body was taken over by Herself, that fucking whore illness, she hasn't even been in control of her tears. She doesn't want to cry but she can't help it, the tears stream from her tear ducts and roll down her rigid cheeks as if irrigating a barren field. Without anyone asking them to come, without being called forth. She chose the cheapest wooden casket. Not only because she's never had much money but so that Rita would rot quickly. Elena never understood why people chose caskets made of noble hardwoods that would take a long time to break down. If so many people believe that we are all of dust and to dust must turn again, why delay the return. They pick fancy caskets just to show off, she thinks, why would they do it otherwise, if they know neither the coffin nor what's inside it are destined to last but to rot, to be eaten by worms, both the wood and that body that no longer holds the person it was, a body that no longer belongs to anyone, like an empty bag, incomplete, a pod without seeds.

Elena sat through the entire vigil, in a plastic chair, beside the casket. *How terrible what happened, Elena,* someone said to her, *my deepest condolences. And what is it that happened,* she asked. Then the person talking went quiet, imagining that Elena preferred not to know, or that medication or grief had led her mind astray. But Elena is not astray. Elena knows. She waits. With her bowed head and her shuffling feet, without seeing the road or what it will bring. She doesn't go astray, even if she sometimes wanders.

Several wreaths were sent. Elena tried to read them but with her bent neck and her tired muscles she couldn't keep her glasses in place. A neighbour came over to read them for her. *Your co-workers from the Sacred Heart Catholic School. Dr and Mrs. Benegas. Your neighbours. Which neighbours?* she asked. The person reading hesitated. *Everyone on the block, I guess, they asked me to contribute at least.* To one side a small palm frond with white flowers and a ribbon that read: *Your friend forever, Roberto Almada.* One of those little palm leaves designed to be placed under the hands crossed over the belly, to make it look like the dead hands were holding them, that they would take them with them on their journey. And she would've had them placed in her hands, if it weren't for the fact that they'd been sent by Roberto Almada. But instead Elena let them sit where the florist had put them, in the corner behind some other wreaths. It was his mother's idea, Elena suspects, which is why it said *friend* and not *boyfriend*, because the hairdresser, just like me, hates the sound of the word boyfriend to describe her over forty-year-old son. Just a little palm, not costing too much. Hard not to suspect it was her when people whisper she even takes a cut of the tips the clients leave for the girls.

As the evening wore on everyone gradually went home. *The souls of the just are in the hands of God and no torment shall touch them*, Father Juan prayed before leaving, *They seemed, in the view of the foolish, to be dead; and their passing away was thought an affliction and their going forth from us, utter destruction.* Elena wanted to stay, foolishly staring at death. She didn't want to go home to rest like a neighbour suggested, *Come back tomorrow, Elena, in the morning when it's light.* As if the morning and the daylight were good things. What did that man know about what the morning meant to her. Forced to open her eyes once again. Daylight signals the start of the fight she has ahead of her, from the moment she tries to get out of bed, pulling on her ropes until her unresponsive back unsticks from the wrinkled sheet, resting both feet on the cold floor tiles, gathering momentum to stand up, dragging her feet towards the toilet where she'll try to sit to urinate, lower her underwear, try to stand, stand, drag her underwear up, tangled, damp, try to straighten it, and then after that, after that, always after that, always a new challenge, as if the struggle just to go to the bathroom on her own in the morning weren't enough. Every morning Elena wakes from sleep to be reminded once again, for yet another day, what awaits her. If it were up to her, she'd have stayed sitting in that chair, in that funeral parlour beside her daughter's body, staring foolishly at death, and she'd pretend that that day, the one she was living, would never end. And that another would never begin. If it were up to her. But the funeral parlour employee insists she leave, saying, *For security reasons the parlour is closed at night. Who holds vigil overnight, then?* she asks. *Times have changed, madam, we have to look out for the living.*

Very early the next morning, after her first pill, she was there again. The first two hours alone, but after nine o'clock the people who hadn't been there the day before showed up, along with those who had been there the day before but who wanted to accompany her daughter to the hole in the ground where she would be deposited to rest eternally. At ten o'clock Father Juan returned to give the eulogy. *The souls of the just are in the hands of God, and no torment shall touch them: they seemed, in the view of the foolish, to be dead; and their passing away was thought an affliction and their going forth from us, utter destruction but they are in peace, hallelujah,* he said and everyone said *Hallelujah.* He's on about the foolish again, she thought, and she wondered who the foolish people the Father was talking about were, if he meant her, who believed that her daughter had been murdered, or if he meant the people who said hallelujah like they said anything else they were told to repeat. Or was Father Juan the foolish one, calling her daughter a just soul even though he assured anyone who asked that Rita had committed suicide, an unpardonable sin for the kind of Christian souls he dealt in. Was Dr Benegas foolish, or Inspector Avellaneda, or the neighbours? Was Rita foolish, or was she? And who was just? *May the Lord have the glory of our sister Rita, that he may take her with him to share in his Kingdom. To have eternal life.* Elena would've liked to believe in glory, and in the kingdom, and in that eternal life. But just as she didn't believe that we are all of dust and to dust we must return, neither she nor Rita could be taken in by a prayer, even if it was a priest praying it. Elena can pray street names, from last to first and first to last, and levodopa, dopamine, dopa, and the dethroned king and Herself and the naked emperor. Backward and forward as many times as necessary. But she can't pray Father Juan's prayer because she'd be lying. And even though it's not her prayer and even though she rejects it, and even though she refuses to repeat it, she knows that she has it inside her, like Herself is inside her. That fucking whore illness. *For Rita's soul, so that the angels in heaven will keep her company. Hear us, Lord. For all the dead, so that they may be called to share the holy Kingdom. Hear us, Lord. For those who remain here on this earth, especially for her mother Elena, so that we may separate from Rita and help her on her departure with resignation and joy, with the same joy she expressed in her time here on this earth.* What joy? Elena thought. Did her daughter express some joy around other people that she never saw? Was she joyful when she was around this priest, around Roberto Almada, who's nodding at everything the priest says? *Let us pray. Hear us, Lord.* Elena didn't know if the Lord would hear them, but she did hear them, and she didn't feel any joy and nor did she recognise any in her daughter lying there cold, stiff, like an empty bag. She did feel resignation, yes, because she knows there's no coming back from death, whether she's placed in an oak coffin or one made of balsa wood, no matter who hears her prayers or whether the one hearing her prayers even exists, whether the entire neighbourhood weeps for her dead daughter or no one weeps at all, there's no possible return.

Shortly after the second pill it was time for the burial. A neighbour helped her get to her feet. The funeral parlour employee closed the wooden lid over Rita's expressionless face and said in a loud voice, *Would the gentlemen who would like to help with the casket please come up to the front?* And Elena heard *the gentlemen* but she went anyway, she didn't bother to ask for permission, she raised her left foot, moved it through the air and when it passed her right foot she set it down, and she repeated the movements, slowly, as best she could but determined, towards the front-left bronze handle of the coffin in which they'd take her daughter to the cemetery, in front of the handles gripped by Father Juan and Roberto Almada, in front of the ones held by the neighbour who gave her the box his 29-inch TV had come in, in front of Dr Benegas and the owner of the private car service on the corner of her street.

They had to wait for Elena to take her place, to turn to face the exit, to straighten her body as much as Herself would allow, to align it with the coffin where Rita lay, to take a breath, and then, with her right hand, the one that responded better, to grab that handle, the first one on the left, the one that wasn't held by any gentleman, and to carry her daughter's casket to its final destination.

7

Sitting on the train that is taking her to the place she hopes to find, Elena watches the trees race past outside the window. She can rest for a moment as the stations slide by and her only task is to watch the trees chase each other in the opposite direction. Trees and houses blur together as if one tree were eating the other, one house eating the next, she thinks. Elena watches it all out of the corner of her eye, the only way she can. She accepts the punishment that Herself, her illness, imposes. At least her eyes are still loyal, although they've lost their expressiveness, they still look where Elena tells them to. But her neck has become stiff, hard as a rock, and it demands total submission. It reminds her who's in charge. Elena's body responds to Herself, forcing her to lower her gaze as if she'd done something wrong and should be ashamed. A few months ago she began to drool since her stooped position made it harder and harder to keep her saliva inside her mouth. *Can you try not to drool on the table while we eat, Mum?* A viscous drool that stains her blouses so that she always looks dirty. Every morning Rita gave her a clean and ironed handkerchief so that the drool wouldn't drip all over the house. A handkerchief like the one she carries in her purse today, which she had to wash and iron herself. But her daughter's attempts had been in vain; she'd find the damp handkerchief wadded up in random places around the house, on the TV set, the kitchen table, beside the telephone, displayed like a trophy or like a souvenir wherever Elena had set it down, without intending to offend her daughter. *Isn't there anything that disgusts you, Mum? Cockroaches,* she answered. Rita also tried to address the problem of the drool using bibs, she found a box of ten for a good price, but even though they were disposable Elena refused to throw the used ones away. *Did you see how much those things cost at the pharmacy?* So she wore a damp and wrinkled blue paper bib smeared with unidentifiable food stains around her neck all day. She'll probably never feel clean again; there's no cure for her illness. There's just palliative care, little tricks to help her do things she can't do anymore, bibs, but no cure. She will be sick as long as she's still alive, and Rita still dead. Till her final days, days like the long one she has ahead of her now which won't end until she finally takes the evening train home, alone.

She travels on. Burzaco, Adrogué, Temperley, Lomas, Banfield, Lanús. Lanús, Banfield, Lomas, Temperley, Adrogué, Burzaco. She travels. She looks out of the corner of her left eye. The trees are still eating each other. Then out of the corner of her right eye towards the aisle as if she needed to make a symmetrical effort. Herself requires her to keep her head down, orders this act of contrition that the muscle enforces and Elena doesn't argue with the order but she mocks it. She doesn't laugh or even feel a sense of pride or bravery, she mocks it in order to survive. She's drooling again. She rummages in her purse for the damp handkerchief which she balls up and wipes across her mouth. She looks up and arches her eyebrows in an expression of surprise but she's not surprised, she's merely trying to look forward by pointing her pupils in that direction. The muscles of her cheeks and eyebrows hurt when she does this. Elena wonders if cheeks are muscles, like the muscle that pulls her head down. She never wondered what kind of thing cheeks were. She'd never had to think about her neck, about her eyebrows, to wonder whether they were muscles or flesh, or just skin, and she doesn't know what they are, but they hurt. Something hurts, some part of her body that wasn't used to making this movement that Herself, the illness, forces her, Elena, to attempt, only to mock her. Because there's no way she's resigning herself to staring at the floor from now until she dies, she thinks. If necessary I'll lie down on the ground and look up at the sky, at the ceiling even, just to defy her, to disobey her, and I'll wait for death to come. Her own. One more act of defiance, perhaps the last. But before that, from now until she dies staring up at the sky, she's going to have to find other ways to rebel if she doesn't want to become a slave to that whore who's in charge. Ropes to help her stand up from different places, more bibs to catch her saliva, foam neck braces to lift her chin, hard plastic neck braces when the foam ones aren't enough, adapters for the toilet seat, more ropes, medications that help her swallow, that keep her from urinating on herself more than she already does, medications that make other medications more effective, or that keep the other medications from destroying her stomach, more ropes. That's why, even though it hurts, she makes an effort with her cheeks and her eyebrows so that her eyes, still loyal, can look at something other than the floor. On the train she never looks straight ahead, it would be too much effort just to see the back of the seat in front of her. After the man who tapped his knee to the rhythm of his music got off, Elena managed to move to the window seat, dragging herself over and holding onto the frame. Her skirt got balled up underneath her but she didn't care; she sat there beside the window, with her head down, moving her pupils from one side to the other, enough to see the trees and the houses racing past in the opposite direction, blurring together, their colours merging into a rapidly moving undefined stain until the train gradually slowed, allowing each image to step forth and retake its original shape as the train finally came to a halt at some intermediate station, before once again repeating its ritual of arrival and departure.

It's been years since she's travelled by train. The last time was when Rita insisted they attend a support group for Parkinson's patients that met once a month in Hospital de Clínicas. But it just made Rita feel worse than ever and she never asked to go back again. It was hard to even find the meeting, they got lost in the hallways that led who knows where, the dark stairwells, the elevators that didn't go up nor down, the people waiting anyway, weary, and banners listing the union's demands hanging out of Elena's line of sight so that Rita had to tell her what they said. The smell. What was that smell? Elena wonders but she can't remember, she can't pin it down. It wasn't death, the smell of death is different, she now knows. She didn't know it when her husband died, because the death of her daughter was the real death. The smell of illness maybe. Of pain. The smell of the future, she thinks. Because, there, they saw for the first time what awaited them. They thought they knew, but that afternoon they saw it. Up to that point Elena had just a slight shuffle when she walked. Like when someone starts walking but they hesitate. That's something that happens to so many people, Elena thought. She thought, but now she knows. She knows what awaits her, her future, because she saw it. Before, with just a little medication, she could get going. And then everything seemed almost normal.

Normal like putting on a jacket without help. That was the first sign, the day Elena couldn't put on the left sleeve of her jacket. Who would've thought that being able to get your arm in a sleeve could be such a big deal, she thinks. Now she knows how important it is. The right one, yes. But the left one, as much as her brain orders her arm to lift, to point the elbow forward, to stretch the forearm back with the palm of the hand up towards the ceiling and into the arm hole and once inside the sleeve to keep sliding down the hole in the fabric to return to its habitual position, her body did not obey. The arm up in the air, the elbow facing forward, the hand searching in vain for the hole and the sleeve hanging empty. Because Herself, the whore, had decreed that her left arm would never again go into a sleeve. That's why Elena adopted the habit of using a little shawl or poncho that her neighbours made fun of and didn't understand until the illness finally made itself evident. Another act of defiance. The shawl was the first defiance, if she remembers correctly. If my arm won't go into a sleeve ever again as long as I live, then there won't be any more sleeves, Elena had decided. And she preferred to let them talk about her behind her back than for them to know the truth. Because for a while the illness had been a secret between Rita, Elena, and Dr Benegas; hidden like a lover. *If you're lucky enough not to shake*, Rita had said, *why go around telling people? They'll just pity you. But if no one sees you shaking no one's going to know you have Parkinson's, and the longer it takes for them to give it a name the better, Mum.* Elena didn't shake, still doesn't, and at that meeting at the Hospital de Clínicas they both realised, she and Rita, that far from being an advantage, not shaking was worse. *Aw, poor thing, you don't shake. They say the patients who don't shake have it the worst, that the Parkinson's advances more quickly,* the lady sitting next to her, shaking like a leaf, had told her.

And the two of them, Elena and Rita, heard her but they didn't say anything, not even to each other. They didn't even feel the need to ask Dr Benegas about it at the next appointment. Because they'd observed the others that afternoon. That was enough. They looked at each of the people around them, the ones that shook and the ones that didn't. Elena couldn't see herself in any of them. She didn't have a vacant stare like the man who told the group how he'd had ropes and railings installed in his bedroom so he could get up in the night. Her fingers didn't wave in the air like she was counting money or dealing an invisible hand of poker. She didn't drool like the woman crying in the first row. She didn't shake like the woman who'd said *poor thing*. She didn't identify with any of them that afternoon, but she knew her fate because she saw the Elena that she would become.

That was the last time she'd travelled by train into Buenos Aires, she thinks. That time she hadn't needed to watch everything out of the corner of her eyes because she didn't yet know that her sternocleidomastoid could turn on her, she'd never even heard its name. If the king had already been dethroned, the news was kept within the walls of the palace. Herself was at work only in the shadows. Secret lover. The messenger arrived with his levodopa in time for every battle. But much more important than all that, Elena wasn't alone on that other trip. Rita was sitting beside her on the train, even if all she did was help her put on the sleeve of her jacket. And she fought with her, quick lashes of dry leather, then she marched off to walk several paces ahead. They'd fought that afternoon too. It had taken Elena a long time to get on the train and Rita had got impatient. She'd been worried they weren't going to make it, so she pushed her through the door. She placed her two open palms on her mother's backside and pushed her hard, almost knocking her over. *Try a little harder, Mum*, she said. *Stop busting my balls*, Elena answered. Because she did try hard and still does, otherwise she wouldn't be sitting now on that other train watching the trees chase each other out of the corner of her eye. But sometimes, Elena now knows, trying hard isn't enough. Rita also knows now, she thinks, if in the place she ended up, the place where we'll all end up, a person can know anything. But that afternoon she'd become furious with her mother. *If you think I'm busting your balls you don't want to even imagine the state mine are in.* And if Elena, with her sternocleidomastoid muscle, and her drool, and the sleeve that won't let her arm in, wants to keep on living, despite all that, she can't believe that her daughter wanted to die. She can't believe it. She is dead, it's true, but she couldn't have gone up that belfry on that rainy evening, she couldn't have tied the rope around the bell yoke and then put it around her neck, she couldn't have made that knot, she couldn't have kicked away the chair she was standing on and let herself hang by her own weight until she died. She couldn't have. She wouldn't have been able to. It was raining that evening. Elena knows it wasn't 'an accident' like Inspector Avellaneda puts it, trying to soften it for her. She never trusted the police. Not now, not ever. But she's alone, and it doesn't matter whether they believe her, she just needs someone, anyone, to listen to what she has to say. The coroner didn't listen to her, or the police inspector. Avellaneda had listened but then they ordered him to close the case and he wouldn't see her anymore during working hours. He did meet her a couple of times at the café on the corner of the police station when he came off duty. *I can only talk to you in an unofficial capacity, Elena*, he had let her know. They'd also met a few times under the ombú tree in the square. But it's been a while since then and anyway he only ever repeated the same story, which Elena doesn't believe, that her daughter committed suicide. Father Juan would still agree to meet in the sacristy, but she's grown tired of those visits. They don't do any good because he just listens to her like someone confessing, and she doesn't need to confess, what she needs are answers to her questions. The director of the Catholic school agreed to see her too, but he just looked at her and listened and nodded his head like he agreed, but he didn't have anything to say besides, *We've planted a tree in Rita's memory, Elena* and what does she care about a new tree. Rita's co-workers won't listen to her, or the neighbours, even the one who cries when she talks to Elena, and says, *I understand, you don't know how much I understand, I wouldn't be able to accept it either,* but who asked her to understand, all she wants is to be heard, for them to try to remember and to report what they know, but no one knows anything, no one suspects anyone, no one can even imagine any possible motive or think of any enemies her daughter might have had. So, since they don't know they just repeat what the police say, suicide. Elena's deaf body is surrounded by deaf ears, she thinks, more deaf than her feet when they won't walk. All of them deaf, deaf people who say they understand even though they refuse to listen, Elena knows. Roberto Almada listened to her at first, and he'd still listen to her if she'd let him. *Don't come by anymore, Roberto,* she told him one afternoon when he dropped in on his way home from the bank and started crying in her kitchen. *It's nothing against you but don't come by anymore.* He had listened to her but he hadn't done anything about it, and nor was he going to. He was the first to accept the theory of suicide, he didn't tell her that, she read it in the report, he said that Rita hadn't been well lately, that she wasn't the same, she wasn't interested in anything, she didn't laugh much. When had she ever laughed much? Elena read Roberto's transcribed words, and she reread them twice to make sure that's what it said, that she hadn't been mistaken, that she didn't laugh much. She didn't laugh much. What would he know, Elena thinks. Deaf. Blind. Even though they can walk, move freely, and do everything she's been robbed of. That's why she's trying to get to Buenos Aires on that train that stops at another station she can't read the name of because the letters are blurred, slanted, in the corner of her unfocused eye. She counts on her fingers and guesses it must be Avellaneda. Like the inspector who will only see her off duty, sitting on the curved and twisting root of the ombú tree in the square.

No one knows as much about her daughter as she does, she thinks, because she's her mother, or was her mother. Motherhood, Elena thinks, comes with certain things, a mother knows her child, a mother knows, a mother loves. That's what they say, that's how it is. She loved and still loves her daughter even though she never said it, even though they fought and kept their distance, even though their words were like cracks of a whip, and even if she didn't hug or kiss her daughter, she felt a mother's love. Is she still a mother now that she doesn't have a child? If it had been her who'd died, Rita would have been an orphan. What name does she have now that she's childless? Has Rita's death erased everything she was? Her illness didn't erase it. Being a mother, Elena knows, isn't changed by any illness even if it keeps you from being able to put on a jacket, or freezes your feet so that you can't move, or forces you to live with your head down, but could Rita's death have taken not only her daughter's body but also the word that names what she, Elena, is?

Elena knows that her daughter was murdered. She doesn't know who did it or why. She can't figure out the motive. She can't see it. So she has to accept it when the coroner and Inspector Avellaneda and Roberto Almada all say it was suicide. And she knows everyone else says it silently to themselves. But it was raining. She's the mother, and it was raining. That changes everything. But she can't prove it on her own. She won't be able to do it by herself because she doesn't have a body. Not now that the dethroned king and Herself are in charge. Even if she uses all the tricks in the book, she won't be able to uncover the truth unless she recruits another body to help her. A different body that can act in her place. That can investigate, ask questions, walk, look directly into people's eyes. A body that will obey Elena's orders. Not her own body. The body of a person who feels the need to repay a debt. Isabel's body. That's why she's sitting on this train, so that this other body, the body of a woman she hasn't seen for twenty years, may help her uncover the truth that her body refuses her. The truth that she can't see. Even if it takes all day to get to Buenos Aires. Even if she is stranded, immobilised every time the pills stop working and she has to wait, trapped inside her body, where time has stopped, again, to count the streets and stations and kings and whores, and naked emperors, backwards and forwards, emperors, whores, kings, streets, stations.

She trudges on, one foot in front of the other, despite the fact that no one can restore the king to his throne, or restore life to her daughter, or restore her daughter to her.

8

From the start Father Juan was one of the least willing to talk about it, repeatedly deflecting Inspector Avellaneda's attempts to meet with him. *Either you're not insistent enough or Father Juan takes you for an idiot, Inspector. You're not saying I should add him to the list of suspects, are you, Elena? I already told you, you have the obligation to investigate all possible theories.* Elena waited for the right time, not too close to either of the daily masses or the hours reserved for confessions, or to siesta. She went to the sacristy and rang the bell. When the priest opened the door he was straightening the collar he wore instead of the robes like they used to. His nap had probably extended as he'd got older and her calculations may have been off by a few minutes. *Come in, Elena*, he said. So she did. *Watch your step*, he warned her, but it didn't do any good, as Elena passed over the threshold the toe of her shoe kicked the wood twice, and on her third attempt the priest approached to help her through the door without falling. *What a coincidence, Elena, I was about to call you, the school wants to hold a service for your daughter Rita, we're going to do it this Sunday during the seven o'clock mass, I'd like you to join us.*

Elena made a mental calculation and determined that 7:00 p.m. wasn't a good time due to her medication schedule, but she nodded her head. Father Juan went on, *How are you dealing with your grief? I'm not dealing with it yet*, she answered. *That's not good, Elena, there's a time for everything, a time for death, and a time for mourning. I don't have time to mourn right now, Father. You have to make the time, Elena, it says so in the bible, in Ecclesiastes, you need to mourn. I'll mourn once I know the whole truth, when I find out who's to blame for how my daughter ended up that day.* The priest looked at her and while he doubted Elena was prepared to listen to what he had to say, he said, *That day holds no mysteries other than Rita's reasons for doing what she did, the reasons she took with her to the grave, Elena. It was raining that day, Father, and Rita never came near the church on rainy days, you never noticed all those years? No, I never noticed, why wouldn't she come? Because she was terrified of being struck by lightning. Oh, Elena, you can't possibly believe that! It wasn't me who believed it, it was my daughter. But she did come here that day, Elena, I saw her body. The Gómez boys found her, you know them, don't you? They're the sons of the owner of the brick yard on the other side of the avenue, cheeky little boys but good kids, they help me with little maintenance jobs around the church and I let them ring the bells to announce the start of mass, they have fun up there, or they used to.* The priest offered Elena a cup of tea, she didn't accept it. *Do you want to pray together? I didn't come to pray, Father, I came to find the part of the story that's missing, up to now the only thing I know is that my daughter's body was found hanging from the belfry of your church. It's not my church, Elena, it's everyone's church, it belongs to the community. What I don't know is how it got there, Father. You know how it got there, Elena. No, I assure you that I do not know. It's hard to accept the death of a loved one and even harder in circumstances like* this with so many mixed emotions. *What emotions are mixed, Father? Pain and anger, because we, as Christians, know that our bodies do not belong to us, that our bodies belong to God, and so we cannot go against Him, and because you know this it is hard for you to accept it, I understand, Elena. Well I don't understand you, Father.* Father Juan looked at her, her bowed head with those terrifying expressionless eyes looking out from beneath her eyebrows and forehead, demanding answers. But Elena didn't say anything, she remained silent, she waited, and then the priest spoke more directly, *The Church condemns suicide just as it condemns any murder, any wrongful use of the body that does not belong to us, whatever name you want to give the action, suicide, abortion, euthanasia. Parkinson's, she says,* but he ignores her. Father Juan walked over to a counter, served himself a cup of iced tea from a pitcher and took a sip. *You're sure you don't want any?* Elena felt like he was trying to stall for time, like a dentist who has already administered the local anaesthesia but when he tries to pull the tooth his patient screams and then he knows that he has to wait a little longer, that the nerve hasn't yet blocked the pain. *Elena, you should try to remain calm, despite the obstacles that the Lord places in your path, you should try to always remain constant in your faith. What faith, who told you I ever had any faith? You tell me, Elena, with your actions. You mean because I haven't killed myself, because I haven't hung this useless body from your bell, or because my daughter died and I'm still here? Elena, please, that's blasphemy, the body is an object that belongs to the Lord and man only has the right to its use. I haven't had the right to the use of my own body for a while now, and it wasn't God who took it away from me, but this fucking whore illness. Elena, please calm down, swearing won't solve anything, I suggest that you pray for your daughter's soul, for God to have mercy on her in the Final Judgement. I don't give a damn about the Final Judgement, Father, I'm interested in judgement here on earth, I want you to help me uncover the truth. You want the truth, Elena? I'll repeat it for you, then, as clearly as possible: your daughter committed an aberrant act, she took her own life, she wasted a body that did not belong to her but to God, she decided she couldn't continue living even though every Christian knows that it is not up to us to decide when our life will end, that's the truth and we have to feel pity for her. It was raining, Father. If you keep talking about the rain, Elena, I'm going to have to conclude that you're committing the sin of arrogance. What are you saying I'm committing? Pride and arrogance, to think that you know everything, even when the facts show something else. But isn't that what you and your church teach every day? We teach the word of God. Appropriating the word of God is the greatest act of arrogance, Father, pure arrogance.* Elena got up with some difficulty, it took her three attempts but she managed to stand without help, and she shuffled to the door. Father Juan watched her curved back, he felt sorry for her and silently made the sign of the cross. After reaching the door, Elena tried to get her foot over the step, but she couldn't raise it high enough. So Father Juan walked over, and in spite of her protests, he helped her. Elena was on one side of the threshold and he on the other. *You need to get someone to shine your shoes, Father,* she said. And the priest looked down at his black loafers, which hadn't been polished in a while. *Ask those boys who help you with church maintenance, your shoes are part of the church, too, Father.* Elena took two steps and Father Juan was about to close the door but before doing so he said, *Oh, Elena, I forget you are a mother.* She didn't turn to look at him but she stopped and said, *Am I a mother, Father? Why would you doubt it? What name do you give to a woman with a dead child? I'm not a widow, I'm not an orphan, what am I?* Elena waits silently, with her back to him and before he can answer she says, *better you don't give me a name, Father, if you or your church ever find a name for me you'll probably just take away my right to decide how I behave or how I live my life. Or how I die. Better not*, she says and starts walking away. *Mother, Elena, you are still a mother, you will always be. Amen,* she says and she leaves with the certainty that she won't ever return.

II

MIDDAY

(THIRD PILL)

1

The train arrives at Plaza Constitución. Elena waits for the other passengers to exit the carriage and only then does she attempt to do so herself. She slides across the vinyl seat, hauling herself from the window to the aisle. The inverse route. The zip of her skirt gets caught on a rip in the seat where yellowed foam has bloomed forth. She manages to pull herself free. She leans on the armrest and stands up. She's glad to note there's still some levodopa circulating in her system. She looks at her watch, it's more than two hours till she needs to take the next pill. She hangs her purse on one shoulder, and presses it to her belly; even though it's been a while since she's ridden the train she knows she can't walk cheerfully down the platform of Constitución station with her handbag hanging off her shoulder. She knows she's easy prey for anyone who might want to grab it from her and take off running. Though it'll be the thief who gets the shock, Elena knows, since her handbag holds barely enough money for her train ticket. But she has her ID and her pills, her handkerchief, the keys to her house, a juice box and a cheese sandwich. Everything she needs to complete this journey. So she presses her handbag tightly to her belly, because if she loses her pills she won't be able to walk. She passes through the open train doors and steps down onto the platform. She shuffles behind the huge crowd being funnelled into improvised lines to show their tickets. A man approaches her and asks, *Do you need any help, grandma?* I'm not your damn granny, she thinks, but she doesn't say anything, she looks at him and keeps going, as if she were deaf too. Deaf like her feet when they refuse to respond. Deaf like everyone who refuses to listen when she says it was raining that evening. The man is probably barely ten years younger than her. Maybe no more than five. But his body isn't shrivelled up like hers is, so he thinks he's a lot younger, he thinks he has the right to offer help. The man looks at her body and calls her a grandma. She could be a grandma at sixty-three years old, but the man who wanted to help her called her grandma because she looked so helpless. She would've liked to have been a grandmother, but she could never imagine Rita as a mother. She'd always suspected her daughter was infertile. Maybe because she was so old when she got her first period, almost fifteen, the last girl in her class to 'become a woman'. And she was always very irregular, very light. *You have stingy periods, Rita. It's better that way, Mum, cleaner.* Rita never stained a single sheet, never once had cramps that kept her from going about her day. As if her menstruation wasn't heavy enough to cause any discomfort. Almost like a simulation, just enough to keep anyone from asking questions. Elena, on the other hand, had always had abundant periods, generous, of the kind that leave no doubt that everything, inside, is working properly. She still remembers the day she stained the seat during a matinee at the movie theatre when Rita was around ten years old. *Get up, and let's get out of here fast, get up right now.* But Rita took her time, she had to gather her bag of sweets, put on her shoes.

I said hurry up and let's go, Elena repeated. *Wait, Mum, what's the big rush? This rush*, Elena answered and she turned her daughter's head to show her the stain on the brown velvet seat. That got Rita moving, she practically ran out of the theatre, crying, but not without looking back to see if anyone else had noticed her mother's stain. Elena was certain that her womb worked just fine, but she'd always had her doubts about her daughter's. If Rita wasn't able to stain like she was, Elena couldn't be sure. When Rita was around twenty Elena took her to see Dr Benegas; she was too old for the paediatrician so Elena took her to her own doctor, who'd also been Elena's mother's doctor. And her aunts' doctor. He saw almost everyone in the neighbourhood. The same doctor who years later would teach them about levodopa, substantia nigra, the sternocleidomastoid muscle, Parkinson's. But that time, when those things didn't yet exist because no one had ever named them, Dr Benegas suggested a test to see if Rita had a uterus. *To make sure we're not in for any surprises, Elena, to check that Rita's not a pod without a seed who won't be able to fulfil her purpose in the world.* Back then ultrasounds weren't what they are now, where you can see everything underneath the skin and flesh like you're watching it on a movie screen. Before, in order to see, you had to get in there somehow. Rita and Elena went to the clinic together. Benegas had two assistants. Rita had fasted the night before, the last thing she'd been able to eat was quince jam and two flavourless crackers. And in the last six hours not even water. She was hungry, but just thinking about that quince jam made her want to gag. They put her on a bed and brought out a device Elena never learned the name of but looked like the kind of pump they use to inflate footballs. Except that they put the valve into Rita. They stuck it into her belly and blew her up. One, two, three, ten times. Rita cried. *Come now, Rita, this can't possibly hurt,* Dr Benegas said. And she didn't answer, so her mother answered for her, *Of course it doesn't hurt, Doctor, she's just trying to make us feel bad.* When Rita's belly was sufficiently inflated they adjusted the bed so her feet were pointing up to the ceiling and her head down, diagonal to the grey tile floor. And they studied her. Rita shut her eyes so she wouldn't see what they were doing. Elena didn't see either because Dr Benegas asked her to leave, saying that the mother and daughter were fighting so much that it put the procedure at risk. *Stop crying, Rita, if this is how you react to some little test I seriously hope you're not able to have kids, if you only knew how much that hurts, right Doctor? Oh, well I wouldn't know how much that hurts,* said Dr Benegas and they both laughed as Rita lay at a forty-five degree angle to the floor, filled up with air. Due to the position of the bed, Rita's tears fell upward, from the tear duct along the curve of her eyelids, tracing the arch of her brows before racing over her forehead and disappearing into her hairline. Rita felt someone rub her hand under the sheet and then grip it, firmly, another hand holding hers. She opened her eyes for a second and saw one of Dr Benegas's assistants standing on that side of the bed, staring at her. When he saw Rita's eyes on his, he caressed her hand with a finger. And he smiled at her. Rita squeezed her eyes shut tighter than before and pulled her hand away from him, pressing it against her side. She waited, stiffly, but no one came for her hand again. A while later she felt them pull the pump from her body and she opened her eyes, the assistant had moved away. *Don't tense up so much or it will be harder to release all the air we put in you,* Dr Benegas said as he pushed on Rita's belly to expel the gas they'd filled her with. And then it was all over, they lowered her down, they showed her how to press on her belly to push out the air that was still left, *If you won't let us do it you're going to have to do it yourself,* and they sent her home. She has a uterus, don't worry, the doctor told Elena before saying goodbye in the waiting room.

Elena would've liked to be a grandmother. If she had a grandson, she wouldn't be walking alone down this platform smelling of old fryer grease, making a trip she hoped would lead her to a body that could help her. Because if she had a grandson she'd be talking to him about Rita, explaining what she was like at his age, what she was like before. And he would ask questions, and she'd make up stories, she'd embellish her memories, invent the child that Rita never was, all for him, for that little boy, the boy who would give her a name, Grandma, even though Rita was dead, and then the smell of grease would vanish. But it doesn't vanish, it fills her nose and envelops her bent body, it sticks to her clothes, it saturates her, as she shuffles along. The loudspeakers announce a delay, the people around her complain loudly, they whistle, and Elena is there, in the midst of the whistling, with no grandson and no daughter. She still hasn't decided whether she'll take the subway or a taxi when she gets out of the station. Because it's eleven o'clock and it won't be time for another pill until after noon, a little while after she's eaten something to make sure the medication will be assimilated as it should be, nothing with too much protein. Dr Benegas told her not to eat protein at lunch, something like the cheese sandwich she carries in her handbag. She gets in one of the lines and lets herself be pulled along by the crowd. She imagines this must be what it's like at the football stadiums when there's a big game. She's never been to a stadium. Rita neither. Maybe, if she'd had a grandson, she would have taken him. She moves as fast as she can. The man taking the tickets urges the crowd along and the people pushing against each other without anyone thinking it's odd that they're being prodded by people they don't know beyond the fact they're sharing the same narrow route. It's Elena's turn, standing next to the man taking tickets she puts her hand in her pocket and rummages wildly with her fingers; she feels along the seam but she comes up empty-handed. The line doesn't back up because there's no one left behind her, but another train is pulling into the station and soon the gates will once again fill with hurrying travellers, anxious to push her or anyone else out of their way just to get wherever it is they're going more quickly. *It's fine, go ahead*, says the ticket-taker before she can find her ticket and he waves her through but she keeps looking. *Go ahead ma'am, go ahead*, he insists. Elena looks at him without lifting her head, straining her eyeballs up to look at him from beneath her forehead, from between her brows. Her eyelids and her cheeks hurt, but she keeps looking at him as she takes her hand from her pocket and holds out the ticket so that he can see it.

2

Inspector Avellaneda is another person who never wanted to see, Elena thinks. *You need to get your eyes checked, Inspector.* Benito Avellaneda accepted the criticism with the same resignation he'd accepted the task assigned to him under precise orders: meet with the mother of the deceased, but make it clear that as far as the police and the courts are concerned the case is closed, it was suicide. *If necessary, offer to arrange psychological assistance for her, Avellaneda,* the inspector had told him, but Avellaneda never had the nerve, for him, a mother, his own or anyone else's, was sacred, and he couldn't just brush her off. Avellaneda wasn't, and never had been an inspector, he was just an officer and the task of dealing with Elena was a punishment, a kind of unofficial probation after being caught in the vault of the Provincia Bank, where he'd been assigned to guard cash transfers, with his pants around his ankles and his penis in his hands, aimed at a female bank teller who was waiting half-naked against a wall of security deposit boxes. *For fuck's sake, Avellaneda, next time be more discreet,* said his superior, and he put him on office duty. Verifying changes of address, taking down noise complaints, filing car thefts, sending complaints to the corresponding authorities, minor violations, background checks, and not much more until Elena's case came up, or rather Rita's, or both. *Tell her you're an inspector, officer, you have my permission,* the chief told him. *That way the lady will think her case matters to us. I feel sorry for the old bird, Avellaneda, you will too, but the case is closed, even if she wants to keep dredging it up and she won't let it go. We're doing enough already, don't you think? We're not obliged to assign an officer to listen to her; we're doing it strictly out of humanitarianism.*

Her meetings with Avellaneda on Mondays, Wednesdays, and Fridays quickly became the thing Elena looked forward to most. At ten o'clock sharp she'd walk into the station and wait for him to arrive. *You're too relaxed for a police officer, Inspector, you're going to be late to the crime scene. That must be why they don't promote me, ma'am,* he said turning red as he remembered the vault at the Provincia Bank where his career had ended, and not because of a lack of punctuality. Avellaneda must have either gained weight or his jacket had shrunk, because he couldn't button the blue blazer he wore with the Buenos Aires Provincial Police shield on it. The collars of all his shirts were frayed. If Elena had seen them she would've offered to turn them over for him like she'd done with her husband's shirt collars, but her range of vision, sitting across the desk from him, didn't extend above his second unbuttoned button. At first Avellaneda felt uncomfortable with the woman staring at his belly, until he realised it wasn't personal, that even if she'd wanted to, Elena couldn't see any higher than that, so as the meetings continued, he learned to suck in his stomach, to hold his breath, or to sink down in his chair so that their faces were at the same level and he could see her face, sitting that way for so long that his back ached.

The first few times they met, Elena had demanded explanations, whether there were any leads in the investigation, expecting answers to questions no one had asked. *She didn't go there to kill herself, Inspector, the rope was already there in the belfry, the chair she was standing on was there, she didn't plan that, someone did it for her.* And Avellaneda just nodded like someone talking to an elderly aunt they visit from time to time, following the conversation without really listening, just there to spend a little time with her. At first they argued. *The thing is that as far as the police and the courts are concerned there's no doubt that it was a suicide, ma'am. But it was raining, Inspector,* she responded, and Avellaneda had nothing to say about the fact that it was raining because for him and his people that was of zero importance. Soon Avellaneda learned to respond, *Yes, ma'am, it was raining,* not denying the rain, but also doing none of the things Elena had hoped he would. In order to pass the time during those interviews he read her pages from the report, sometimes accidentally rereading pages they'd already argued over weeks before. Elena quickly realised that there couldn't have been any leads because there was never even any investigation. So she started bringing in her own clues. Rita's diary, which no one had asked to see, her address book, a list of all the people who knew her daughter, written out in her handwriting, distorted by the illness. *If there's anything you can't read, let me know, Inspector. Don't worry, ma'am, I can read it,* the officer replied as he held the piece of paper Elena had given him and wondered how long it had taken the woman to get all those twisted blue letters onto that sheet of lined notebook paper. A list of the last places her daughter had been on the days leading up to her death. To Roberto Almada's house, the Catholic school, the supermarket, Roberto's mother's hair salon, the offices of the health insurance company where she'd gone, once again, to demand a reimbursement for a renal exam Elena had done two months prior and which they still hadn't authorised. *Let's see if we can get you to stop smelling like piss, Mum. To Dr Benegas's office*, Avellaneda added. *When was my daughter at Dr Benegas's office? Two days before her death, didn't you know? No, she didn't tell me about that. She might not have told you but she was there, Elena. But she wasn't sick. She didn't go for herself, she went for you. I didn't even have an appointment with Benegas. She went to talk about you, Elena. Inspector, you don't suspect Dr Benegas, do you? No, of course not, I'm just saying that if you want to make a list of all the places your daughter went before her death you have to add that she went to see Dr Benegas, if you want it to be complete. Of course I do, Inspector. Maybe she said something to him, to the doctor. You do suspect Dr Benegas, don't you Inspector, don't lie to me. No, Elena, I'm just saying that your daughter was also there, if you want I can add it, if not I'll leave it out. You can add it, Inspector, you're the one who has to investigate, that's your duty, I'm just a mother. Whatever you think is best, Elena*, the officer answered, but he didn't seem to have any desire to add anything to the list. So Elena took the page from his hand, she leaned across the desk to pick a pen from the pencil holder, and she added Dr Benegas's office to the bottom of her scribbled list. Then she gave the list back to the officer. *Here, Inspector*, she said, *do your job, and do it properly.*

3

Elena decides she'll take a taxi; she crosses the busy station blindly dodging obstacles. Like a swimmer who can only see the bottom of the pool, she tries to stay in the lane she's staked out for herself. But the others don't see her lane and they cross into it, coming and going from all directions. The more observant ones stay out of her way, the unobservant bump into her. She continues on, as if no one else existed, just like she feels no one else knows she exists. But they do exist, they pass in front of her, they move away, so many pairs of feet. And Elena keeping to the lane that only she can see. Someone crashes into her and apologises without waiting for her response. Another person steps around her but the backpack hanging from their shoulder smacks into her, brutal and uncaring. A group of feet form an imperfect circle a few yards outside her path. Poles that probably hold signs, or banners or flags. Poles that hold up demands. Unpaid salaries, firings, street vendors who don't want to be displaced, Elena doesn't care, she holds a sign with her complaints on it too, it's just that no one sees it. Someone shouts through a megaphone, and the circle applauds. Someone mentions God, some god, and the Son of God. Another long line of shoes, shoes worn by people waiting for a slip of paper to verify that the train they arrived on was delayed, once again, so that their wages won't be docked. A taxi will be better than the subway, she thinks, as she's enveloped by the imperfect circle of shoes and the voice speaking into the megaphone, and the people applauding the voice, or God, or his Son. A taxi will be better than the subway. Not because the subway only goes as far as Carranza and from there it's still ten blocks, like they told her at the private car service on the corner of her street. A taxi will be better than the subway because in half an hour she won't be able to get up from the seat, any seat, whichever one she's settled her body into. And she doesn't want that to happen in the subway tunnel. Even though it's been a long time, years, since she's ridden in a taxi, she still remembers how to do it. She recalls having watched the empty subway cars disappear into the tunnel at the terminal, before another train appeared on the opposite platform, ready to make the return journey. She doesn't know if it was the same train. She'd never cared before, but now she might sit down and not be able to stand up again when she wants to, so now she cares. She knows that the train will eventually come out of the tunnel that swallows it because otherwise the subway system would get backed up with trains. But after how long? Later that afternoon? At the end of the day? Before the next pill starts to take effect? Or after? Elena's time is different from the time kept by trains, running underground from one station to another. She doesn't have a timetable. Her time is measured in pills. The different-coloured pills she carries in her handbag, in the bronze pill box with several compartments that Rita gave her for her last birthday. *So you don't mix them all up*, she told her and set the box on the table. It wasn't wrapped, just stuck inside a clear plastic bag, with no name on it, like the kind you get at the grocery store, but thinner and without any label. *What about the candles?* Elena had asked. So Rita rummaged in a kitchen drawer until she found a used candle, the ones they kept in case the electricity went out, lined with drips of wax, filthy with grime from being forgotten so long at the bottom of a drawer, stunted, cracked in half but held together by its wick. Rita pulled the blackened wick upright, brushed it off with her fingertips and lit it. She held it out to Elena and said, *Blow.* And Elena blew, twisting her head and lips to the side to reach the candle, drooling onto the Formica table top. *How is it possible that you can't keep your handkerchief with you, Mum.* The flame flickered slightly, *Blow again, Mum,* and Elena once again pursed her lips to one side, tried to inflate her cheeks and gather more air into her mouth, to aim for the target, to stretch her neck a little closer to the candle, and she would have blown it out this time, but a drip of wax fell onto Rita's hand at that moment, *Goddammit,* her daughter said, shaking the candle in the air, one, two, three times until it went out, and Elena just swallowed all that air.

If she couldn't stand up when it was time to get off the subway, she would disappear into that black tunnel where she doesn't know what goes on and, what's worse, where Elena doesn't know how time is kept. That other time so different to that time she keeps without clocks. Like a state of limbo, she thinks, a place where nothing goes either to heaven or to hell. Either heaven or hell would be preferable to being stuck there halfway, it always seemed like the worst option to her. Limbo or purgatory, she can't remember the difference between the two but she knows there is a difference, and that she, at one time, knew it. She wonders whether today, on her way to Isabel Mansilla's house to talk about her dead daughter, if the fact that she can't remember is significant. The word purgatory sounds funny to her because she purges, every day, her body is a walking purgatory, that sometimes, for brief periods, walks. She has to purge herself with laxatives, ever since Herself made her intestines lazy. *It's not that your intestines aren't working,* Dr Benegas said when she complained about the number of days she'd spent without being able to go to the bathroom, *Parkinson's patients have lazy intestines, Elena, but it's nothing that can't be solved with some prune juice every morning or a nice plate of greens for lunch.* Purging. That's why, even though she doubts whether heaven, hell, or purgatory even exist she wants to take a taxi. She exits the station and looks for a taxi rank. She asks in a newspaper kiosk. *Which way are you going?* the newspaper seller asks her. And Elena can tell that the man has looked at her and has understood. Because it doesn't matter which taxi rank will send her off in the direction she needs to go. What matters is finding the closest one. As close as possible while her body can still respond, can still shuffle along. Before it turns off and leaves her stranded alone and immobile in this strange city. Alone, without a body. What can you do if your body won't obey? Elena wonders this as she drags her feet in the direction the newspaper seller indicated. What's left of you when your arm can't even put on a jacket and your leg can't even take a step and your neck can't straighten up enough to let you show your face to the world, what's left? Are you your brain, which keeps sending out orders that won't be followed? Or are you the thought itself, something that can't be seen or touched beyond that furrowed organ guarded inside the cranium like a trove? Elena doesn't subscribe to the notion that a person without a body is a soul, because she doesn't believe in the soul or in eternal life. Even though she's never dared to admit that to anyone.

She barely even admitted it to herself, once she was unable to lie anymore. Because Antonio, her husband, had been a practising Catholic, and he wouldn't have understood, and on top of not understanding he would've been upset, all those years working at the Catholic school, not only as the porter but also as the theology teacher, and finding out that his wife, the mother of his child, didn't believe in the soul or in eternal life. Foolish, Elena now knows he would've called her, because that's what Father Juan called her the day of her daughter's funeral, her or anyone who looked at death as final, as if there were nothing else after our earthly life. Maybe that's why Rita had been so ambivalent and cold towards her faith. Because she was raised by one fervent Catholic, and one who only pretended to be. That's why Rita wore a cross around her neck but skipped mass if it was raining, because she was more afraid of lightning than of the double offence she was committing by lying and not going to mass. And she didn't confess all her sins, just some of them. And she didn't pray every night. *There are days He doesn't deserve my praise*, she said. But she visited seven different churches every Good Friday, and she fasted and abstained not only on Good Friday but also on the Thursday, and on Ash Wednesday, and every Friday of Lent. She wore a new pair of pink panties every Christmas even though she knew that it didn't have much to do with the Church's precepts and the Gospels, and she bought a pair for her mother, too, but Elena always ended up exchanging them for black ones, *Why would you think I can wear pink panties, Rita? What's the big deal, no one besides me is going to see them, Mum*. She never went into church with her shoulders uncovered. She never bit the communion wafer. She fasted for an hour before taking communion. She always arrived at mass before the Creed so that it would count. She made the sign of the cross every time she passed a church. As if her religion were based more in the rituals, in the folklore and traditions, than in the dogma or faith. Rita, in her way, had God, a God of her own who she put together like a puzzle with her own rules. Her God and her dogma. Elena didn't. Then why do those words that aren't part of her prayer still float around inside her head? Why does she keep thinking about heaven and hell, about resurrection, the Creed, forgive me my Lord and I am repentant, penitence, sin, and in the name of the Father? Words yes, but not God or dogma. There's not even a body, now, she thinks, and she's thinking about herself but also about Rita, buried underground. Two dead bodies. Hers, and that other that was once inside her, feeding off her, breathing the air that she breathed. A body made of dust and turned again to dust, like it says in the Gospels. The body of her daughter. If only she could believe in the soul and in eternal life, and that we are all of dust and to dust we must return, she thinks, but Elena knows that the only dust we will return to, time and again, is the dust covering her shoes as she climbs into the taxi and says straight down 9 de Julio to Libertador, down Libertador until it turns into Figueroa Alcorta, and then straight on to the Planetarium and left to the Spanish Monument, and then retake Libertador to Olleros. And even though she doesn't give the exact address the taxi driver knows where to go, or at least he knows enough, because without asking any questions he leans over the passenger seat, almost as clumsy as her, to turn on the meter and he puts something away in the glove compartment. Elena knows this because even though she can't see him she hears him move and because her vision is suddenly darkened like a cloud has passed in front of the sun shining through the front windscreen. The man sits back in his seat ready to set off but stops, just in time, because in the rear-view mirror he sees that the back door is still open. Elena has just finished settling her handbag into her lap, but she hasn't shut the door yet. She's only got one of her legs inside, rumpling the paper floor mat from the carwash the man took his taxi to. She can't get the other one in, she hasn't been able to move it, she points her knee outward, her foot hovering in the air waiting for Elena to place it on the floor using both her hands. The man gets impatient, *Do you need help? No, that's not necessary*, says Elena, and using the leg that's already inside as leverage, she lifts the other one in, rotating it at a right angle like a turnstyle and then she pushes hard down on her thigh until her foot hits the floor. Then she knows she's in. The taxi driver asks if she's ready and she stretches a little further, grips the handle and pulls the door towards her body with all her strength, as if it were the rope she used to stand up every morning. *Ready,* Elena says, *let's go*. She imagines the taxi driver looking at her in the rear-view mirror, looking at the roots of her hair speckled with grey and the little flecks of dandruff that Rita complained so much about, *Use the dandruff shampoo, Mum*. Embarrassed, she makes an effort to raise her head and look at him. But time, Elena's time, has stopped. There's no more levodopa to help her move. Nothing. Elena knows. She knows she has a wait ahead of her, a few minutes until she can take the next pill and then the time it takes the medicine to dissolve and begin to move through her body. The wait, that time that is measured without clocks, with her prayer to keep her company. The prayer about Herself, and the messenger, and the dethroned king, and the naked emperor, the streets between her house and the station, and the others that still lie ahead of her, the train stations she's just left behind, levodopa and dopamine, the muscle, and then again Herself, the king, the dethroned king without a crown, naked.

The car moves, and Elena is thankful there's someone to move it for her.

4

*A*dd *the two women who work at the health insurance office to the list of suspects, Inspector Avellaneda. You really think that's necessary, Elena?* the officer asked, beside her on the curved root of the ombú tree in the square. It was after they'd stopped meeting at the police station. *We did more than humanly possible for that woman, Avellaneda, and the people in the neighbourhood are beginning to talk,* the chief had said a few days before. *What are they saying, Chief? They're saying we're taking money from her, Avellaneda. Assholes, how could they think we'd do that to an old lady? That's how their minds work.* But the officer didn't have the nerve to tell her not to come back. For her sake, but also for his own. By that point meeting with Elena had become the task he most enjoyed, like a chore taken on grudgingly that ends up becoming an important ritual. Avellaneda was surprised to find himself looking forward to their meetings, given how little he'd been able to do for the woman. He made up an excuse, *they're having my office painted, you'll see how good it looks, Elena.* And Elena didn't believe him, but she went to meet him in the square anyway, and she talked to him there like she believed his lie. *Rita treated those two girls at the health insurance office very badly,* she insisted. *Well,*

Elena, that doesn't sound like enough of a motive. Seriously, I'm telling you, very, very badly, do you understand, Inspector? I understand, but you don't just kill every person who treats you badly, if so, how many of us would be left in the world, I'd have to kill more than one boss I've had, not in the force, on the building site, I worked as a builder before this, Elena, did I tell you that? No, you didn't. And my brother, first my brother and then my bosses, my brother would have to kill his father-in-law, my sister-in-law would have to kill my mother. Even though I'm a bachelor, I'm not sure I'd still be alive, said the officer. *You would, Inspector*, Elena assured him, *You seem like a good person. Don't trust appearances, Elena, the uniform can be deceiving. Don't be silly, Inspector,* Elena says, laughing, *that uniform isn't helping you. You are a good person, Elena.* But Elena shook her head, *You say that because you never saw me fight with Rita. I'll add you to the list, then*, said the officer, in an attempt at humour, but the second it was out of his mouth he knew it was stupid and inappropriate. *Why not, Inspector*, she answered, *You have to investigate everyone, I'd be thrilled if you did, even if you started with me.*

Rita's interactions with the women at the health insurance office became increasingly tense as Elena's illness got worse and the expenses that needed to be reimbursed grew. Elena had witnessed multiple examples of mistreatment. Her daughter's blatant mistreatment of the insurance agents and their polite mistreatment of her, disguised behind soft voices trained specially in the Central Office. Their tone of voice didn't help, Rita always got angry with people who spoke quietly. *I don't trust them, Mum.* They said she'd maxed out the expenses allotted for physical therapy, that the prescription said five hundred but the insurance only covered three hundred. *Three hundred what? Pills.* That the generic brand the doctor had prescribed didn't match the medication he asked for, that a treatment wasn't covered by the plan that Rita had paid religiously for the two of them for twenty years. *Have you tried to get it through the public medical service, PAMI?* They hadn't tried with PAMI, they'd avoided all mention of the public medical service ever since they'd waited over an hour for a PAMI ambulance to help Antonio who lay dying of a heart attack on the kitchen floor in the house where Elena now lives alone, only for it to finally arrive five minutes after he'd died. The siren wailed down the street, getting closer and closer to the house, but Elena already knew it wouldn't do any good. They did try at what had been previously called the Institute for the Lame, which the mother and daughter still called by its old name; it had been changed years ago to avoid offending anyone but the new name was exhausting to say. *Go to the National Services for Rehabilitation and Promotion of Disabled Persons, on Ramsay street, Rita, and get her a disability certificate, that'll simplify things for you a lot,* the girls at the insurance office had told her when the expenses began to multiply astronomically. But Rita didn't see the need, *What good would it do? Well for example every time you bring in a request for physical therapy I have to get it authorised by an auditor at the Central Office and that takes time, also in the case that they do authorise it, I have to discount it from your allotted quota, then your physical therapy runs out, do you understand? No, I don't understand. Let me explain then, with the disability certificate you don't have that limit on treatments and everything's much quicker. What will the next limit be and why do I have to go somewhere to certify that my mother is disabled, are you blind?* The girl lowers her gaze. *Look at her, I dare you,* Rita demands. *What do you think?* The employee looks up but doesn't respond. *Isn't this enough? It's not for me, I know your mother well enough by now, I need the certification in order to...* But Rita interrupted her before she could finish, *Do you really think she needs a certificate to show she's disabled, why would you ask for something so obvious? It's for the Central Office, they need the piece of paper. And you're not able to tell them no. Even if I tell them no, they'll ask for it anyway. It's not enough for you to tell them, her medical chart isn't enough to prove it, the letter from her doctor isn't enough? Those are the rules. Tell them I'll bring her in there, parade her in front of anyone who doesn't believe us, so they can see her, but you can't make my mother suffer through more of this bureaucracy.* None of their pleas changed the paperwork required by the Central Office. So off they went, to Ramsay street, fourteen months later. *You're giving me an appointment for next year?,* Rita asked the secretary at the front desk of what had been the Institute for the Lame, which to her surprise was an old, much-extended mansion set in tree-lined grounds. *There are no earlier appointments? There are a lot of people who need the same thing. Well I hope those people are still alive fourteen months from now.* When the date of the appointment finally arrived Roberto Almada got the bank to give him the day off and to lend him a car. *Is it really necessary to bother that man, Rita? Tell him he doesn't need to put himself out for me. He's doing it for me, not you, Mum.* They got there on time, both women in a bad mood, especially Rita, who was sure there would be some problem, some little thing that would mean she'd have to come back again, a piece of paper that was missing, a signature, a stamp, some miniscule requirement that when revealed to be lacking would suddenly become of utmost importance. But that's not what happened. They waited a little while, Elena told Rita she'd prefer for Roberto to wait in the car, *We wouldn't want them to think he's the one here to get certified as lame, Rita.* And Rita, despite being furious at her mother's comment, must have had similar worries because she sent him outside without any argument. They sat in the waiting room surrounded by other people seeking the same certification. A couple holding hands and taking turns cuddling their baby with Down's syndrome, an elderly mother dragging along a daughter who covered her face with her handbag like she was some famous actress who didn't want to be photographed, a man in a wheelchair who was missing both legs. Elena stole glances at them, made up back stories for them based on the shoes they wore, the movement of their feet if they were able to move them or their stillness if they couldn't, and when she couldn't gather enough information from what she was able to see or what her imagination was able to fill in she would ask Rita about them. *Shut up, Mum, would you like people to talk about you like that?*

There were ramps everywhere, all the offices had signs showing the name and title of the person they'd find inside, on the walls were posters with step-by-step instructions on how to complete the process. In any event, they didn't wait long at all before they were seen by a female doctor who within three minutes had looked through the folder containing copies of Elena's ID, her health insurance card, the last receipt from her retirement pension, the medical chart they'd had Dr Benegas's secretary make a copy of, the completed and signed forms, and without even looking up at Elena signed the piece of paper that from now on would tell anyone who wanted to know that Elena was disabled. Parkinson's, she wrote on the page. *Is that it?* Rita asked when the doctor handed her the paper. *Yes, that's it*, the doctor said, *Your mother's case is very clear, it leaves no room for doubts. It's just that they always make us jump through so many hoops, Doctor. Here? No, not here, but the insurance company, the hospitals. Well yeah*, the doctor agreed, *They want you to get exhausted and give up, don't let them win*, she said. *I won't, doctor, don't worry. Before you leave don't forget you can get a sticker for your car, and our legal advisor will be*

able to answer any further questions you might have. They
didn't have a car, so they didn't need the parking permit
or the license plate registration fee waived, but they went
to see the advisor. They shared the room with the couple
who had the baby with Down's syndrome and a girl who
was there with another girl who was blind. The lawyer
told them that the first thing they should do was get their
certification laminated, and to keep it under lock and key.
*You wouldn't want to have to go through all this red tape all over
again.* Elena thought that, even though she couldn't see
his face, the lawyer must be a handsome man, and a nice
guy since he was worried about her and the time she'd
invested in that process. *Those of you who want the parking
sticker and the exemption from license plate registration fees can
apply today,* said the legal advisor, and Elena knew that he
was looking at everyone even though she couldn't see
just like the blind girl couldn't either. *Law 22,431 protects
your rights, here are the phone numbers you can call if you have
any questions,* he said, pointing to a line on the model
certificate that he then circled in blue pen on each of
theirs. *And the most important thing I have to say to you is
that from here on out, no one, at any health insurance company
or any hospital, can try to charge you or refuse to authorise your
medication or the treatment you need for the disabilities that you
suffer, since starting today those expenses aren't covered by them,
but by the State.* This sentence made it clear why the health
insurance company couldn't just look at Elena to see her
disability. Payment upon delivery. The lawyer shook each
of their hands, Elena hid her wadded up handkerchief
inside the sleeve of her sweater and held hers out too.
She would've liked to sit a while holding that soft strong
hand, but Rita rushed her out, saying, *Let's go, Mum, the
doctor has to shake everyone's hand,* and she pulled her by
the shoulder and guided her out. As they were leaving,
the doctor called out to the couple with the baby, *Stay for*

a second, I want to talk to you. He's nice, I told you he was nice, she said to Rita, but her daughter was several steps ahead and didn't hear her.

Elena walked out onto Ramsay street crying, when she got into Roberto Almada's car he asked her, *What's wrong Elena, why are you crying? They treated me kindly, son,* she said, and couldn't say anything more.

After she received the disability certificate the fights with the girls at the insurance office became less frequent, they couldn't refuse everything anymore since someone else was picking up the tab, and that meant that Rita had fewer reasons to let rip at them. Until that afternoon when she asked them to authorise the two boxes of Madopar. Dr Benegas was going to be away for a conference and he didn't want Elena to run out of medication. She handed the prescription to the girl who usually helped her. *This prescription doesn't say continuous treatment. So? So I can't authorise two boxes if it doesn't say continuous treatment. The prescription says two boxes. Yes, it says two boxes but it doesn't specify continuous treatment. There's no cure for Parkinson's, how could it not be continuous? You have to ask the doctor to write continuous treatment in those exact words. You can shove those exact words up your ass. I'm just doing my job. Obedience is no excuse, if your superior gives you an idiotic order and you obey, it's because you're an idiot too, and I regret to inform you that idiocy also requires continuous treatment even if no one will write it out for you in those exact words.* And then Rita ripped the prescription out of the girl's hand and left the office in such a hurry that she left her mother sitting in the waiting area. None of the girls dared to say anything. They just stood there behind the desk, and Elena opposite them, stooped over, head down, drooling onto the shirt she'd bought with her last pension cheque. Elena imagined that the insurance company girls must be uncomfortable with her sitting there, opposite their desk, so she tried to stand up but she couldn't. The phone rang, neither of the employees answered it. Elena rocked forward and with an effort was able to stand, gripping the arms of the chair. But the chair began to slide out from under her and Elena with it, and one of them unfroze and ran to catch her. In that moment the door opened and Rita barged in, *Don't you dare touch her*, she said, the employee let go and Elena wobbled again. *Let's go*, her daughter ordered. *I wish I could*, Elena answered.

5

Elena lets herself be driven along. She decides to take her medication early. She knows it's okay, that even if Herself, that fucking whore illness, might not like it, Elena can manipulate her time with pills, although only barely. She opens her handbag, rummages inside and pulls off a piece of the cheese sandwich she packed before leaving home, she knows the pill is easier to swallow when it's mixed with the wet crumbs, which is why she carries that piece of bread and cheese beside her wallet and keys. She chews, swallows, some crumbs fall to the floor of the taxi and Elena tries to cover them with the paper mat before the driver notices. When she finishes chewing she opens her handbag again, she finds the pill case and the juice box, she rips the straw from its wrapper, she takes the pill, pinched tightly between her thumb and index finger, and places it in her mouth, as far back as she can. She holds it in place with her tongue. She stabs the little straw into the juice box and drinks. The pill won't go down her throat, it won't go past her tonsils. She takes another sip. The taxi driver is talking to her, she ignores him, breathes in deeply through her nose to keep from suffocating. A honk startles her, then another. *Idiot*, the driver says, and if Elena could see she'd know he was referring to the man who didn't make it to the other side of the avenue before the light changed. *But if I run him over I'm the one who'd have to pay for being in the right.* Elena takes another sip, pressing the box to make the juice come out faster and even though the pill doesn't move it begins to dissolve from all the liquid. If she could just lean her head back a little she'd be able to swallow it, but she can't, her body won't permit that little shake of the head everyone else does to swallow an aspirin. So she leans sideways on the seat, she slides down to help the pill get over that hill it can't climb, and this time she manages it, the pill scrapes down her throat and disappears. In relief, Elena drops onto her arm, straightens the juice box so that it doesn't spill, lays on her side across the seat. She waits. Someone walks up to the car and tries to clean the front windshield. Elena can see the squeegee through the space between the seats, but the taxi driver honks his horn, repeatedly, until the hand wipes away the detergent it had splashed onto the windshield and disappears. Elena can't see who the hand belongs to, probably a kid because it was a small hand, because it wasn't wrinkled, but these are merely guesses, from her position she can only be certain of what she sees on the dirty roof of the taxi that is driving her. *What animals*, the driver says, and Elena doesn't have the courage to ask who the man is referring to, so she remains silent, tries to move the arm she's lying on so that it won't go numb under the weight of her body, she manages to shift her weight and feels proud at her small victory over Herself. The taxi driver turns on the radio and she hopes it will keep him from talking, but she's wrong, because the radio host only riles up the taxi driver. The driver begins to rant with even more fervour, angry, gesticulating in his rage so as to leave no room for doubt. *That's exactly how it is*, he agrees with the radio announcer, looking for Elena in the rear-view mirror. *Did you drop something? I dropped myself*, Elena answers. *Are you okay? I'm okay, I'm okay*, Elena replies from her inclined position. *Do you need help? No, no, I already took my medication. Do you want me to pull over? No, I want you to keep going. You're not about to hurl, are you? Hurl what? To vomit, ma'am. Of course not, sir, I'm ill, that's all. What illness do you have? Parkinson's*, Elena says. *Oh, Parkinson's*, he repeats. *They once told me I might have that but no, it was the drinking, the shakes I had were from the drinking, I like to drink. Oh, how nice*, Elena says. *But my wife gave me an ultimatum, quit drinking or take a hike, that's how women are, final, they think they're in charge, and you let them think it, anyway when I'm working I don't drink, almost never when I'm working, but I like to drink, what can I do.* And Elena thinks that she doesn't know if she likes to drink, but that she never does. She thinks about the wine she doesn't drink as she watches a spider walk from one seam in the roof of the taxi to another. She should've got drunk at least once in her life, and learned how to drive, and worn a bikini, she thinks. A lover, she should've had a lover, because the only sex she ever knew was the sex she had with Antonio, and that had been a point of pride, having been only for one man, but today, old, stooped, lying on her arm, knowing there will never again be any sex for her, Elena doesn't feel pride, she feels something else, not sadness, not anger, she feels an emotion she doesn't have a name for, the feeling you get when you realise you've been foolish. To have saved her virginity, for who, to have been faithful, for what reason, to have remained celibate after becoming a widow in hopes of what, believing what? Virginity or fidelity or celibacy means nothing now, lying there on the back seat of a taxi. Not sex either. She wonders if she could even have sex if she wanted to. She wonders why she doesn't want to, if it's because of the Parkinson's, because she's a widow, or her age. Or because she's so out of practice after so long without even thinking about it. She wonders if a woman with Parkinson's who wanted to have sex would be able to. She laughs imagining herself posing the question to Dr Benegas at her next appointment. And a man with Parkinson's? Could a man with Parkinson's make love? Would he be able to penetrate a woman? It must be harder for a man, she thinks, because he can't just lie there and let it happen. Does a man who's ill like her have to time sex around when he took his pills? She feels sorry for this unknown man, she's sympathetic, she's glad she's not a man. The radio begins to play a bolero and the taxi driver hums along. *Bésame mucho*, the song goes and the driver echoes it, *como si fuera esta noche la última vez*. Then he realises he doesn't know any more of the words so he switches to humming and then starts talking again about wine and drinking. *My wife is going to kick me out if I keep drinking*. The last alcoholic beverage Elena drank was a strawberry-flavoured sparkling wine that Roberto Almada brought over the first time he came for dinner. It was the 'official introduction', even though they'd known each other forever. *Who'd have thought that the little hunchback would end up being practically family, huh Rita? Don't call him a hunchback. It's not an offensive term. Of course it's offensive, Mum. Do you want to see if he gets offended?* Roberto and Rita were united by their convictions more than anything else, that way they both had of stating the most broad, arbitrary, clichéd notions as absolute truths. Convictions about how another person should experience something they themselves had never experienced, how people should walk through life along the roads they'd walked down and the ones they hadn't, issuing decrees about what should and shouldn't be done. Their first, their deepest connection, branded with fire in a secret pact that joined them together, was their mutual fear of churches. And in Roberto's case the terror wasn't limited to rainy days, he feared them under all climactic conditions. He'd had the problem since he was little, from his time in Lima. His mother, Marta, or Mimí, as she'd started calling herself when they'd returned from Peru, had followed a boyfriend there, a tango dancer who was not Roberto's father, who'd given a free concert at the Sports Club where she tended the bar on Sundays and bank holidays. She took the boy with her when they moved, *She had to, who else would've taken him? His hunchback was obvious even as baby. That's enough Mum.* And shortly thereafter the tango dancer had got sick of them both and kicked them out without a peso to their names in a country they had no other connection to than his mother having felt horny. So she learned how to do hair, before she'd only done manicures, and she rented a room in the Barranco neighbourhood from a classmate at the beauty school where they taught her how to style, cut, and dye hair. The logical thing would've been for them to come home, but she wasn't willing to admit her failure, and returning so soon would've made it all the more obvious. So even though in Peru she could barely make enough to feed her son, she stayed there in that city perpetually swathed in clouds, where it never rained, where the ocean was a daily reminder of how small they were. The years passed by unnoticed as the boy grew and with him his hump, and while his friends took girls to the Bridge of Sighs to whisper lies about eternal love, he went every other day to the same bridge, alone, to look up at the Chapel of the Hermit, where they said the bell had once fallen during an earthquake and smashed open a priest's head. A stain on the pavement, picked at random by whoever was telling the story, had been left by the priest's spilled brains, marring the ground for all eternity. *If you misbehave the headless priest will take you*, said the old lady who watched him while his mum went to work or did whatever she did. And Roberto grew up terrified not of the priest, because he didn't even know how to misbehave, but terrified of bells, constantly calculating the probability that another one might fall and kill someone, always standing back far enough to make sure he wouldn't be the one decapitated. It didn't matter to Roberto that there had never been an earthquake recorded in all of Greater Buenos Aires, he still didn't want to go too near any church. That's why Roberto couldn't have killed Rita and hung her from the bell, because aside from the fact that he would've been no match for Rita, who was so much stronger than her beau, Roberto also never went near any church, Elena knows. The police cleared him of suspicion in any case, but for other, less transcendent reasons. He'd been at the bank all day participating in an internal audit, doing a cash count, with more than twenty people who could confirm his alibi, the police chief had told her when she insisted that it was murder, that they should look into suspects and motives. *You don't have anyone to help you, ma'am*, the driver asks her as she watches the spider disappear through the half-open window. *No, I don't,* Elena says. *You're all alone in the world? Yes. Son of a…! And the rest of us complain. I had a daughter but they killed her,* Elena hears herself saying almost without thinking. *You just can't live in this country, ma'am, we get killed just for going out on the street, that's the way it is,* says the driver. But she lets the driver draw his own conclusions from her words, *I had a daughter but they killed her,* and she doesn't care who the *we* is that the driver includes her as part of. Elena just wants him to be quiet for a little while, to play another bolero, so that she can concentrate on the task at hand, on moving this body that, for a while now, she knows, has not belonged to her.

Even though Elena doesn't see the taxi move down Libertador past the Hippodrome, it's noon and she knows that the sun must be directly above her, heating the roof of the car. A bus braking loudly beside them startles her, but immediately she realises that everything's fine, that it was just a noise, that a noise doesn't mean anything more than that, and she goes back to concentrating on the fact that in several more blocks she'll have made it to her destination and the body she's trapped inside will have to move, to get going again. She tries to give it the order and make it listen. From her horizontal position she raises her right foot, just a few centimetres, she lowers it, then the left. They both respond, she tries again, right foot up, then down, left foot up, down, and again, one more time. Then she rests, despite the fact that she won't be able to sit up without someone giving her a hand, she knows she's ready, that when the taxi arrives at her destination she will only need a point of leverage to be able to pull herself up, a hand, a stick, a rope, and once again she'll be able to walk, one foot in front of the other, for a while, between one pill and the next.

6

Mimí couldn't have killed Rita either, Elena knows, which is why she never suggested that Avellaneda add her name to the useless list. She must have wanted to, Elena thinks, but it's not a crime to want to kill someone, not even if that person is your child. No one can go to jail for thinking or feeling something, only for doing it, and even then only sometimes. And Mimí didn't do it, although she probably wished Rita dead at some point, for threatening to take away, over her dead body, the only thing she had in the world, that hunchbacked boy who loved her unconditionally, attached to his mother like an infected appendix no one dared to remove. Mimí couldn't have killed her because Elena was with her at her hair salon, before, during, and after the moment that Rita was hung from the church bells, exhaling the last breath that would ever enter her lungs.

It had been Rita's idea. Elena never would've thought to waste an entire afternoon of her life in that place lined with mirrors and yellowed old posters of women with outdated hairstyles. She didn't want to spend time in that hair salon or any other. Rita worked hard to convince her mother to go to the appointment she'd made for the wash, cut, dye, styling, manicure, pedicure, and waxing. And she'd made the appointment around her medication schedule, so that Elena's body wouldn't be without levodopa. *Just go and stop complaining, you're going to feel much better when it's over. But I don't feel bad, it's only my toenails that bother me, and you can cut them for me next week. That's true, Mum, even though I think it's disgusting, I can cut your toenails, I could even do it today, but then what? What do you mean? After the toenails, then what? I don't know how to dye or cut hair. Is all that necessary, Rita?* Her daughter glances at her briefly before saying, *Have you looked in the mirror, Mum?* No, Elena answers. *Well, it shows, go and stand in front of a mirror some time. I stand in front of the bathroom mirror but I can't see myself, I can only see the tap and the sink. Take the mirror down off the wall, Mum, and put it in front of your face, look at yourself and then you'll understand. Why do you care so much about how I look, Rita? The problem isn't how you look but who has to look at you. I'm the one who has to look at you, every day, Mum, I help you out of bed every morning and see your toothless mouth, your expressionless eyes, I have breakfast, lunch, and dinner across from you, watching your drool mix with your food into a disgusting paste, I put you to bed at night and I bring you a glass of water so you can put your teeth inside it, but it's hard for you to get them in so I have to touch them, to pick them up and put them in the glass with my own hands, I go to sleep but the day doesn't end there because a few hours later you'll be calling for me to take you to the bathroom, and I take you, I pull down your underwear, I pull it up, I don't have to wipe you, that's true, I won't wipe you, that's too much, but I sit you on the bidet and hand you a towel, and I hang it up to dry, I flush the toilet so the water will carry your urine away, I lie you back down in bed, I tuck you in, you stare at me from bed, toothless, with your eyes that look constantly surprised and your whiskers sticking out of your cheeks like wires, and I'm about to leave when you call me back, again, to arrange your feet, or the sheet, or the pillow, so I go back, I see you again, and once again I smell that stench of piss that never goes away completely because it's you, because it has saturated your skin, and I hear you take your hoarse, snoring breaths, I turn off the light on your bedside table and I see your teeth again, the ones I put into the glass myself, with my own hands, I wipe them off on my pyjamas, but they still smell, like you. So the problem is me, Mum, the problem is that I have to look at you. And that's going to change if I go to the hairdresser? No, you're right, if it were up to you nothing would ever change, but you're going to go anyway and you're going to change.* And she dragged her to the beauty salon and left her sitting on the wicker chair in the waiting area. She was more surly than usual and didn't say hello to anyone, not even Mimí. *I'm leaving her here*, she said, and she left. Elena sat still, waiting, her eyes on the woven rug that clearly hadn't been cleaned in months, peppered with hair of all colours. On the coffee table was a pile of tattered magazines that had been new at one time, and another pile of flyers for natural foods, royal jelly, aloe vera patches and other products of the kind that promised to improve the health of anyone who tried them. Except her, Elena knows, for her there was no hope. She stretched out her arm and grabbed the closest magazine, she flipped through the pages pretending to read while she waited. The stuck-together pages turned a few at a time, so Elena wet her index finger to separate them, which was bad manners but Rita wasn't there to scold her, to say, *Don't be disgusting, Mum. Can't you see that the Parkinson's makes it hard for me to turn the pages, dear? Don't make up excuses, Mum, you've always done that, don't blame the disease for things that are no one's fault but your own.* There was music playing in the background, an attempt at a piano concert garbled by the speakers hung in the corners of the salon. The smell of shampoo and conditioner mixed with the smell of hair dye and hot wax to create a strange aroma. Elena couldn't decide if it was pleasant or not. It just smelled the way it smelled. A girl came to get her when she'd almost finished flipping all the pages of the magazine. *Come along, grandma. Grandma my ass*, Elena answered, and then laughed before the girl had time to react. She'd learned a long time ago that hiding an insult inside a joke would cancel out any anger. *Grandma my ass*, she repeated, and held up her hand so the girl could help her up. The girl pulled but not hard enough. Another girl came over and pushed Elena from behind, grabbing her under her shoulders, saying that she knew what to do because she'd taken care of her grandmother until the day she died. Once they got her standing, even though it wasn't necessary, they each took one of her arms and guided her to the chair, like they were a walking armrest. The hair colour was first, they covered her chest with towels, then slipped a black plastic cape over her, open at the back. *Are you sure you can't raise your head even a little, Elena?* Mimí complained. And Elena tried, but no sooner had her head raised up a tiny bit than it fell back down to where it always hung, where Herself, that fucking whore illness, told it to stay. She sat for twenty minutes under a dryer with a current of hot air hitting her directly on the back of the neck. Getting the dye off her hair in the sink was the hardest part. It took three of them together, one holding her, another holding her neck and pushing her back, another waiting with her arms open not doing anything, as if her job were to remain alert, ready to avoid any possible catastrophe. It was impossible. Despite the precise instructions Mimí gave from where she sat on the stairs leading up to the massage parlour. She ended up getting mad at her employees and trying to do it herself, but that didn't work either. Finally they brought over a bucket and poured water over her head using a tea kettle, which they had to refill twice, Elena took deep breaths between the streams of water, until the water that fell into the bucket she held on her lap ran clear. *I'm tired, let's save the rest for another day*, Elena suggested. *No, no, no*, said Mimí, *I don't want to get in trouble with my future daughter-in-law*. She was lying, Elena knows, since she didn't care about making Rita mad. *Rita asked me to give you the works and you're not leaving here until you're looking brand new. Brand new*, Elena repeated. *Do you want to rest a minute on the massage table? No, thank you. One of the girls can loosen you up. I said no.* Offended, Mimí took her by the arm and sat her in the chair, she detangled and styled her hair in silence and only after her anger had been erased by hundreds of brushstrokes she said, *I hope they make us grandmas.* And once again Elena didn't believe her, if there was one thing this woman didn't want, it was for her son to be taken away by Rita and for a child to be born of that union. *Rita's forty-four*, Elena pointed out. *So what?*, Mimí replied. *I don't think she's going to be able to make anyone a grandma. Oh, don't be silly, Elena, didn't you see on the news how a woman gave birth at age sixty-five? I'm almost sixty-five, I'm a year and a half away, but…* Elena said, trailing off, and everyone went silent. *I'm almost sixty-five myself,* she said again but Mimí didn't dare to say anything, neither did anyone else, although they were all surprised by Elena's age, which didn't match her body. They changed the subject, Elena stopped listening. It was clear that the woman who gave birth might've been her same age but she didn't have the same body. Could a woman with Parkinson's give birth, she wondered. Would there be room in her bent body to house a child? Would she be able to push? Could she breastfeed? Would the medication she has to take harm the foetus? She wondered if when Rita was born she already had that whore of an illness inside her without knowing it, like a seed, waiting for fertile soil in which to germinate. She thought about the illness like a child of her own body. She wondered if her daughter carried that same seed inside her and if one day it would germinate and her daughter would suffer the way she suffers. A useless question because even though Elena didn't know it yet, by the end of the afternoon there would be no seed capable of germinating inside her daughter's body.

The waxing was the easiest part, the girl just crouched beside Elena with a stick smeared in hot wax and, as she placed her left hand on Elena's forehead, she pulled her head up with her right hand and spread the wax on her upper lip turning the stick like someone kneading dough. It didn't hurt, but some of the little hairs remained and the girl insisted on plucking them out with a pair of tweezers. *That's not necessary, child.* And Mimí herself did her hands and feet while Elena watched the woman work, bent over in front of her, almost at the same height. That woman doesn't want my daughter to marry her son, just like I don't either, she thought. Deep down we're alike, and she laughed at how surprised Mimí would have been to hear it, if Elena had dared to say it out loud, to say that Mimí was anything like her.

By the time the woman was placing Elena's feet in the hot water, Rita was probably already hanging from the church belfry. And as it was getting late, Mimí's assistant cut Elena's hair and styled it while she was getting her pedicure. *You'll have to excuse us, Elena, but if not we'll never get out of here.* When she was done they helped her stand, once again the three of them. *You have to come more often,* Mimí said, *your feet are a disaster, how do you ever wear sandals with those heels? I just put them on,* she answered, *or Rita does it for me when I can't. At least put some lotion on them at night, Elena, that helps with the roughness.* And even though Elena showed no concern for the roughness of her heels, Mimí said, *I'm going to send you some calendula cream with Roberto*. It'll just go to waste, Elena thought, because she wasn't willing to add any more chores to the unending list of daily challenges: walking, eating, going to the bathroom, lying down, standing up, sitting in a chair, getting up from a chair, taking a pill that won't go down her throat because her head can't tip back, drinking from a straw, breathing. No, she definitely wasn't going to put calendula cream on her heels.

Mimí guided her to a full-length mirror. *Take a look, Elena*, she said, *you're a whole different person*. And Elena, so as not to be disagreeable, turned her head to the side and tried to look at herself. A strand of hair had fallen right over her eye, but one of the girls, meticulous about her work, rushed to pin it back with a clip and some hairspray. She was able to see a little, enough to compare her body to the body of the woman beside her, the woman who was deep down a lot like her, just a year or two younger. *How do you think you look, Elena? Old.*

7

The taxi turns onto Olleros as Elena indicated, and carries on for two blocks. *It's two or three blocks, I don't remember*, she tells him, and the driver turns right as soon as he gets to a street running in that direction. *Tell me if you see a wooden door with bronze fittings*, Elena says, still lying on the back seat with her eyes on the roof of the car. *Any other clues, ma'am? And a clinic or doctor's office*, she adds. *I'll tell you everything I see, ma'am: a green-grocer, estate agent's, apartment building, Mexican restaurant, like we need any more foreign food than we already have*, the man complains and then continues, *a 24-hour kiosk, a bar, and the block ends. No clinic. Any bronze fittings?*, Elena asks. *Hold on, wait, hey, man, is there a clinic around here? A clinic?*, repeats the voice of the person the driver has asked. *Around here, not that I know of, there's a hospital on José Hernández. No, it has to be on this block or the next one*, the taxi driver insists. *No, not around here. And any bronze fittings?*, Elena asks, but neither the driver nor the voice answer, but the voice shouts, *María, is there a clinic on this block or the next one? Or a doctor's office*, the taxi driver adds. *There was a doctor's office years ago*, a woman's voice answers. *No, María, when was there ever a doctor here? Before you came. I've been here ten years. Well then it was eleven years ago. Where? Where the Mexican restaurant is now. You see? They push the doctors out and replace them with that crappy food*, the taxi driver complains, and the voice responds, *We were lucky the people who live next door didn't want to sell, if not, they'd have put up another tower like they did where the parking lot was. We're going to have to stick all those cars from all those people, where the sun don't shine.* The taxi driver parks in front of the Mexican restaurant, the yellow curb indicating that parking is not permitted. Beside the restaurant, a wooden door with bronze metalwork that can just barely be seen. *You're going to have to help me out*, Elena says. The man looks back and holds out his hand, but quickly realises that won't be enough. He opens his door and gets out, huffing. He walks around the taxi but stops and goes back to remove the key from the ignition, *Can't be too careful these days.* He opens Elena's door, holds out his hand, and she grabs onto it, but he doesn't pull, he waits for her to do so. *Pull*, Elena says, and she moves her arm to show the man what he has to do. The taxi driver understands and he pulls. She stands, wobbling, using the headrest as a lever, though it tilts over and the taxi driver pushes it back into its correct position with his free hand as he helps her out onto the pavement. Elena straightens her clothes, opens her purse, and asks, *How much do I owe you?* The driver bends down to look through the window and tells her it's $22.50. Elena opens her purse and finds a twenty and two twos, *Keep the change*, she says. *Thank you*, the man responds and then asks, *I can get going then? Yes, of course you took me where I needed to go*, Elena says, still standing exactly where the driver placed her. The man walks around the front of the taxi and sits down. As soon as Elena takes her first step the taxi driver starts the engine and forgets all about her. Elena doesn't see him go, but she can picture him, humming another bolero or talking to the radio announcer, complaining along with him, shouting insults and honking the horn because the person in front of him doesn't move fast enough and he isn't able to get through the intersection before the red light.

Elena moves to the inside of the pavement, in front of the Mexican restaurant, and follows the wall in the direction that the taxi came from, dragging her feet. The warm brick scratches her arm but she doesn't mind, because she's finally made it, she's here. When the wall of the restaurant ends a wooden door with polished bronze fittings and a bronze knocker appears. Elena takes a few more steps and she reaches the door, she caresses it, running her hands over the bronze as if she were polishing it, closing her fist around the ring of the knocker, because it's the same one, the same one that Isabel held onto that afternoon, begging, pleading, *Don't make me go in there*, and Elena is grateful that in twenty years no one thought to change the knocker, because it's thanks to that, thanks to this door knocker, Elena knows that she's found the place she set out for this morning on the ten o'clock train.

III

AFTERNOON

(FOURTH PILL)

1

Elena met Isabel twenty years ago, when Rita dragged her into the house one afternoon. It was cold, Elena was knitting beside the heater; orange peel in a pot of hot water perfumed the house. The door opened abruptly, as if Rita had kicked it open, her hands occupied with supporting the woman. She walked in backward, first her body and then the other body, the one she was dragging. *Who is that woman?*, Elena asked. *I don't know*, her daughter answered. *What do you mean you don't know, child? She feels bad, Mum*, Rita said and she half-carried the woman into her room and lay her on the bed. The woman was sobbing but then fell silent: she'd fainted. *Bring me a bucket, Mum.* Elena brought her one and Rita put it on the floor beside the woman's head. *In case she needs to vomit again*, she said. Then she went to the window, closed the wooden shutters, and turned on the light. *Should I call the doctor?*, Elena asked, but Rita didn't answer, she went back over to the woman, dumped the contents of her handbag on the bed, and started going through it. *What are you doing? Looking. For what? A phone number, an address. Why don't you just ask her? Because she can't answer, Mum, can't you see she can't answer?*

She's crying, Elena said. *Yeah, she's crying, now.* A tube of lipstick rolled across the bed and Rita caught it before it fell to the floor. There was a box of Valium, a wallet, several slips of paper, two envelopes, loose change. Elena walked over to the bed, still in control of her own body, twenty years ago, without shuffling her feet, her head high. The woman cried, hugging the pillow, covering her face with it. Elena asked again, *Who is this woman? Why did you come back?* And this time her daughter explained. Rita had found her on her way to work at the Catholic school, on her way back from having lunch with her mother like she did every day, walking quickly to get there on time, to ring the bell that signalled the start of the afternoon classes, but she never made it to ring the bell, because there was Isabel, on the other side of the street, on the checkerboard-patterned tiles Rita refused to set foot on, the ones she wouldn't let Elena set foot on either. Isabel, gripping a tree, was bent at the waist and vomiting. Rita gagged and sped up trying not to look at her. The image disgusted her, but gradually her disgust gave way to something else, she didn't know what, something that made her stop. *A voice, Mum, I heard a voice calling me, she's going to go in there, she's pregnant, it said, and she's going to go in. So I turned around, I went back, I offered her help without stepping onto the pavement. And she said no, thanks, I don't need anything, but she was still vomiting. And I told her, you can't even walk in the state you're in. And she said, I don't have to go far.* She had a piece of paper with an address in her hand, and a name, *you know the name, Mum, Olga.* So Rita said, *Don't do it, you're going to regret it. What do you know? All the girls who come here regret it. How do you know? I know. Mind your own business. It's a mortal sin. I don't believe in God. Think about your child. I don't have a child. You're going to have one. No. You have a life inside of you. I'm empty. When you hear its heartbeat you're going to want it. How do you know? Don't kill it. Go away. Don't kill your child. There is no child. Yes there is. There can't be a child without a mother. You already are a mother. I don't want to be a mother. This woman told me she didn't want to be a mother! Can you believe that? But I told her, that's not your decision. And she had the nerve to ask whose decision it was, and I shouted at her, you have a child inside of you! I don't have anything inside me, she said again, but I was persistent, its heart beats, I said. And she said, there can't be a child without a mother. Don't kill it. Shut up. You'll have to live with your guilt forever. I won't be able to live at all if I don't. None of the girls who do it ever forget. You can't force someone to be a mother. You should've thought about that before. I've always thought it, I never wanted to be a mother. But you are a mother. No, I'm not. They hear babies crying every night. What do you know? The aborted babies cry inside their heads. I'm the one who cries inside my head. Don't kill an innocent being. I'm an innocent being too.* Then the woman covered her mouth and vomited again and Rita saw the wedding ring on her finger. *You're married? That's right. There's a father, mum, do you see? And what does he say?, I asked her. I don't care what he says. He has the right to have a say, he's the father, or is he not the father? Mind your own business. If he finds out he'll kill you. He already did. You can't go against God's will. I don't know anything about his will. He knows, you don't have to understand, just trust. I don't want this thing that's inside me. Don't call it that, I told her, give your child a name. And she keeps arguing, she said again that what she had inside her wasn't a child, and that there had to be a mother for there to be a child, and that she didn't have anything inside her, but then she vomited again, I could tell she was dizzy and that gave me the idea, I told her, you're going to be a mother, and I could tell she was still dizzy so without saying anything I took her by the arm and brought her here.* It wasn't hard, the woman was exhausted and Rita was determined. She dragged the woman away from that place. That afternoon, Rita, who was not a mother and never would be, forced another woman to become one, applying the dogma she'd learned to another woman's body.

One of the two envelopes that fell from Isabel's handbag held the lab results that confirmed her pregnancy and the other was an electric bill in her name, Isabel Guerte de Mansilla, and an address. Soldado de la Independencia. Rita read the address twice. It was the first time she'd heard the name of that street. *Have you ever heard of a street called Soldado de la Independencia, Mum?* But Elena hadn't heard of it either. The streets they knew were all named after founding fathers or countries or battles; they couldn't remember ever having heard of a street named after an anonymous person, someone without a name who had to be referred to by what they'd done. Woman who vomits. Woman who stops abortion. Woman who watches the woman who stops abortion of the woman who vomits. Independence Soldier. What soldier? What independence? Rita got a taxi, it wasn't easy, twenty years back there weren't private car services on every corner, people did other things for work, when someone lost their job they simply found a new one. She locked the woman inside her bedroom. *Get changed, Mum*, she told Elena and she left. Elena went to the closed bedroom door, to listen, maybe if she'd heard the woman sobbing she would've gone in, but no, so she went to change like her daughter had ordered, so that she wouldn't get angry with her too. Rita went to the train station, to what twenty years ago was the only taxi rank in town, and she got one to drive her back to the house. She got out and went to bring the woman from the bedroom. *Help me, Mum*, she said as she struggled to lead her outside, and Elena helped her. Through the open window she gave the driver the envelope with the address, she put Isabel in the back seat and had Elena get in after her. Rita went around and got in on the other side, saying *Wouldn't want her to try to jump out and kill herself and the child.*

The taxi took off with the three women in the back seat. The route took them past the place where Isabel and Rita had met, the pavement in front of Olga's, the midwife, the abortionist, the pavement with black and white checkerboard tiles. *There's no child*, the woman said again as she sat sobbing between them and clenching her fists so hard that when she opened them Elena could see the marks left by her fingernails.

There is no child, she repeated the whole way there. But Rita and Elena ignored her.

2

She raises her arm above her lowered head and rings the doorbell. She waits. Someone looks at her through the peephole, but she doesn't know it and the person looking out can't see her, because Elena is much lower down, hunched over, staring at her shoes, waiting. Keys turn in the lock, the door opens as much as the chain will allow. *What do you want*, says a woman's voice behind the door. *I'm looking for Isabel Mansilla*, Elena responds. *That's me. And I'm Elena, Rita's mother, the woman who twenty years ago*, but Elena doesn't get the rest of the sentence out because Isabel undoes the chain, opens the door, and lets her in. She knows Isabel is looking at her, instead of asking what she's doing there she's trying to figure out why she shuffles, why she doesn't lift her head, why she has to wipe her saliva with a damp and crumpled handkerchief. *I have Parkinson's*, she says to save the woman from having to ask. *I didn't know*, Isabel says. *I didn't have it yet when we met, or if I did I didn't know it*, says Elena as she moves to the couch where Isabel offers her a seat. She wonders why she says she *has* Parkinson's when she doesn't have it, it's the last thing she wants to have. She suffers it, she curses it, but she doesn't have it, having it implies a desire to keep something close, and she desires no such thing. Isabel helps her sit. *Would you like a cold drink? Or a cup of tea? Tea would be nice, but with a straw please.* Isabel goes to the kitchen. Elena watches her out of the corner of her eye. The furniture is stylish: Gobelin upholstery, curved legs that end in a kind of hoof like a goat or a lamb. If she knew anything about furniture, Elena thinks, she'd be able to tell which Louis they were. Or if they were a Louis at all. But she doesn't know, and she doesn't care. A vase sits on the coffee table beside some books on travel, cities she will never see. On the mantelpiece, two framed pictures. Elena cocks her head to the side and tries to see the pictures, straining to lift her gaze high enough. One of the frames holds a picture of Isabel, her husband, and their daughter. A photo similar to the one Rita received every December for the past eighteen, nineteen, or twenty years, Elena can't remember now. No, not twenty, because it was twenty years ago that they came to this house to bring Isabel home. Rita kept all the cards in a folder, organised from oldest to newest. It would've been easy to put them in order without even looking at the date on the back because the girl grew with every new picture, exactly one year older, and the parents grew older along with her, their faces adjusting to the passage of time marked by their daughter. The three of them always smiling, the man in the middle with his arms around the two women. The card was always signed by Dr Mansilla, saying *Thanks for bringing a smile to our faces, eternally grateful, Dr Marcos Mansilla and family*, and the date. Maybe one of the cards Rita kept was the same photo displayed on the mantel. When she gets home, this afternoon, after all the travelling, Elena is going to check. Pink blouse and two pigtails, she's going to check. The other photo is of the daughter and a man. A man, who can't be her husband, Elena thinks, because the girl is practically still a child and the man is older, around Dr Mansilla's age, but maybe he is her husband, because these days, but she stops before finishing her thought because Isabel comes in with the teacups, a teapot, and two straws, one metal and one plastic. *I brought both*, she says, *so you can choose*. Elena chooses the plastic straw, but she cuts it with the knife on the plate beside the coffee cake, she folds it in half and slices across it, *Shorter is better*, she says, and she takes a sip through it.

They both wait for the other one to begin. *Would you like some cake?, Isabel asks, I made it, banana cake. No, thank you. How old is she? Who? Your daughter. Julieta?*, Isabel asks and she glances at the framed picture, *Nineteen, she turned nineteen three months ago. Rita died three months ago*, Elena says, and Isabel starts, *I didn't know*, she says. *That's why I'm here, that's why I came*, Elena explains. Isabel sits silently, not looking at Elena, not even looking at anything in the room but looking back in time, to a place Elena can't see, even though she's been there. Elena feels the need to fill the silence with details. *She was found hanged, in the belfry of the church two blocks from our house.* Isabel grabs the edge of the chair to steady herself, Elena hardly notices, from her hunched position she can't pick up certain subtle movements that happen above the height of her chest, she can only see that the woman across from her has stood up. *I'm going to get a glass of water*, she excuses herself and leaves the room.

Elena sits alone for more than ten minutes, she tries to get up but once again the levodopa has begun its downward swing and she has been stripped of the ability to move freely. It's too soon for the effect of the medicine to have worn off and even though she knows that her time isn't measured with clocks she looks at her watch; it's more than an hour until her next pill, so it's better for Isabel to take her time, she thinks, since her time that isn't measured with clocks has begun to run out like sand slipping between her fingers, like water, and, Elena knows, she won't be able to get off that couch until after she takes her next pill. Through the door that Isabel left ajar a Siamese cat enters and saunters over to the couch where Elena sits. It jumps onto her lap. *Get out of here, who invited you to the party*, she tells it, and gives it a shove. The cat doesn't fall; it begins to walk along the back of the couch, passing behind her hunched shoulders. The hairs on the back of Elena's neck and arms stand on end when the animal brushes up against her. It walks down the armrest and advances onto her, rubbing its head on her hands, butting them, demanding to be petted. *You're better off dead than with me*, she tells it, and the cat seems to understand but it persists, it meows, it rubs against her hands again, but Elena still refuses because she hasn't touched a cat since before she was married, her husband never let Rita have one, not even when he found the kitten she had hidden in a box under her bed, secretly feeding it milk. *No, Rita, cats are filthy animals, they lick up their own vomit and they lick themselves. It's tiny, Dad, it doesn't know how to lick. In a little while it's going to grow and it's going to be just as disgusting as any other cat. I like cats, Dad.* But then he told her about mange, and eczema, and fungal infections, and illnesses that causes babies to be born blind or mentally defective, and again about the vomit they lick up and how they lick themselves until Rita said, *Enough, Dad*, and she decided she didn't like cats anymore. Eventually Rita herself was the one who said cats were filthy because they lick up their own vomit and they lick themselves with the same tongue. Elena doesn't know if she stopped liking cats when Rita did, or if she never liked them, or if she actually does like them. All she knows is that they never had cats in the house because her husband wouldn't allow it, and

Rita inherited his right to ban them, and Elena hasn't touched one since. But the house she's in now isn't hers, and Isabel's cat is insistent, now butting against Elena's feet, moving between her legs, in and out of spaces it shouldn't be able to fit through. If Rita could see me now, she thinks, and Elena knows what Rita would say if she could see her, she knows the lecture by heart but would like to hear it, would like to even hear her scolding and her insults and her anger. She'd choose Rita's insults over her absence any day but she knows that it doesn't matter what she'd choose because death has taken away her ability to choose. Her daughter is dead. The cat jumps back up onto her lap, walks over her thighs, one leg and then the other, circling, watching her from some place behind those blue eyes, and Elena knows what she's going to do. She's going to end up petting it. She's going to give in to it, so that it stops pestering her, so that it will leave her alone. She rubs her right hand, the one that works better, on the animal's head and the animal writhes with pleasure. *You like that*, she says, and she thinks that she might like it too. If she could. If her husband's and her daughter's words didn't leap to mind, saying cats are filthy, if she was deaf like her feet, she could maybe enjoy petting this animal, the tickle of its fur. If she could, if she let herself, but she doesn't. *Cats are filthy, they lick up their own vomit*, her dead husband says to her dead daughter, and her dead daughter repeats it to her, and she listens, as if they were there, her dead family speaks to her, scolds her, gets angry with her, and Elena pushes the cat away so she doesn't have to listen to them anymore.

But the cat doesn't go away, it's not enough for her to move her hand and say, *Go away, kitty, go away*. The animal glances at her and then jumps back up. It can't hear the voices that speak to Elena, and it's not scared of them. The cat feels warm curled up in her lap and he falls asleep and now that she doesn't feel guilty, since she tried to listen to her daughter and her husband, in spite of herself, or maybe not, she lets it lie there.

Sorry, says Isabel, and she sits back down across from Elena. *Is the cat bothering you?* And Elena says no, but now that she's said it, now that she's openly accepted the animal, the cat wakes up at the sound of their voices and jumps from her lap to the floor, abandoning her, leaving her warm lap to once again grow cold. Isabel returned with makeup on, blush and lipstick, but Elena doesn't notice. *I had to get a drink of water*, but surely she drank the water to wash down something else, a tranquiliser perhaps, because she moves more slowly, and she smiles, and she looks as if Elena hadn't just told her ten minutes ago that Rita was found hanged from the bells of a church. *To what do I owe the visit, then?*, she asks and cuts a slice of cake that she has no intention of eating. *What brings you here?* Elena begins with the afternoon that a police officer knocked on her door to tell her that Rita was dead. Before the man even began to speak Elena already knew that something bad had happened. *If a police officer comes knocking at your door, it's a bad sign*, she says and the woman nods her head. *I was sitting there waiting for my daughter to see me all dolled up, cut, dyed, and waxed, Rita had got me an appointment at the beauty salon, I didn't want to go, but once it was all done I wanted to show her, to make her happy, so that she would know that when she went to tuck me in bed that night she wouldn't have to see the whiskers around my mouth that she complained so much about, or my grey roots. But Rita never saw any of that, she never saw me again.* Elena did see her daughter again. They took her down to identify the body. *On the way to the morgue they told me what had happened, your daughter hanged herself in the church belfry, ma'am. It can't be her then, I told them. She still had marks from the rope around her neck, her skin was purple and scratched from the old rope, her eyes were bulging and her tongue was hanging out, her face all swollen. She smelled like shit. She hadn't got lucky according to what the forensic doctor told me, if she'd been lucky she would've broken her neck and died instantly, but her bones were still intact, she died slowly, by asphyxiation, and people who are hung and die of asphyxiation have seizures and they shit themselves. I didn't know that, of course, how could I know that.* Elena takes a sip of tea through the straw, repeats the process two more times before continuing. *Shit, my daughter's last breath smelled of shit.* Isabel stares at her, rocking slightly in her chair. *They say she killed herself, but I know she didn't,* Elena says. *How do you know?,* Isabel asks. *Because I'm her mother, it was raining that day and my daughter never went near the church on rainy days, don't you see?* But Isabel isn't sure if she does see what the woman is trying to say, so she just stares at her, and instead of answering, she asks a random question to fill the silence, *Do you want to put the teacup down? No, I still have a little left,* Elena replies. *But it must be cold by now, don't you want me to pour you a fresh cup? No.* Isabel serves herself, she warms her hands on the cup, swirls the liquid, watches it settle, and then finally takes a sip. *I kept on top of them to follow any possible leads,* Elena says, *I wrote out a list of suspects for Inspector Avellaneda, Inspector Avellaneda is the officer they assigned to the case, but everyone it could've been was somewhere else the day my daughter was killed, I don't have anyone else to add to the list, they tell me to give it up, even Inspector Avellaneda says so, but I tell myself no, that if the person who killed her isn't on the list it's because I don't know them, and if I don't know them the universe opens up, it could've been anyone, and if it could've been anyone, the investigation is going to get harder, I'm going to need to move around, interview people, find clues, possible motives, dates, facts, evidence.* Elena wipes the drool hanging from her mouth and stares at the hooved legs of the table in front of her. She's out of breath, she hasn't talked so much in a while. Isabel waits, lets her take her time without rushing her, not breaking the silence with even a sigh. After a moment Elena is able to resume the conversation. *So for everything that's coming I need a body, but I don't have one, this one just barely got me here, today, I don't know if tomorrow I'll be able to even move, there's not much more I can do, with the Parkinson's, you know? Yes, I know, you told me,* Isabel says. *So I can't control my body. Herself's in charge, fucking whore illness, excuse my language.* Isabel excuses the language and asks again, *So what brings you here? To call in a debt,* Elena responds. *To call in a debt,* Isabel repeats, staring hard, *I knew it.* She smiles nervously, covers her face and shakes her head as if she were trying to prove to herself she's not dreaming. *I knew that sooner or later you or your daughter would come,* she says. *So you'll help me then,* Elena says. Isabel seems confused, *I don't understand,* she says. Elena tries to explain, *Are you going to repay your debt?* Isabel stands up and takes a few steps that don't lead her anywhere, walks back, looks at Elena, asks, *What debt are you talking about? You know,* Elena answers. *No, I don't know,* Isabel says. So Elena spells it out for her, *Maybe you'd like to help me, because of that day twenty years ago when my daughter, without even knowing you, helped you, saved you, a voice called her to do it, so maybe you feel indebted and would like to return the favour; I didn't want to come here and start demanding things, but I thought I'd take advantage of your feeling of owing my daughter something that you could pay back by lending me what I don't have, a body, a body that's able to help.* Elena stops, she's said what she came to say and even though she didn't ask any questions she waits for a response. Isabel doesn't say anything. The two women sit in silence until Elena begins to feel uncomfortable so she continues talking, *Thanks to my daughter you have your daughter, you built your family, you can ring in every new year holding onto them tightly as we see in those photos you send us. Your story had a happy ending, but I've been left with no one to hold onto, and it's not like I hugged my daughter much when she was alive but the fact that I can't do it now, because she's dead, because her body is in the ground, and we are all of dust and to dust we must return again, as my husband said, well that hurts. It hurts.* As Elena speaks, Herself begins to take control of her tongue and her words come out clumsily, some syllables clenched into senseless sounds that the other woman can't make out. Isabel serves herself more tea, takes a sip, stares at Elena, but she doesn't speak, she decides not to speak for the moment, just listen. The cat jumps back up beside Elena and then begins to walk along the top of the couch. Isabel watches it pace behind Elena's hunched back, following it with her eyes. She senses that the animal bothers the woman who sits bent over across from her but she doesn't intervene, she doesn't remove it, this time she doesn't even ask Elena if the cat bothers her, she just watches, the cat and then Elena, observing this woman who rang her doorbell to call in a twenty-year-old debt that she hasn't forgotten. Isabel hasn't forgotten the debt either, but she remembers things differently. She sets the teacup on the table and now sees Elena from a different perspective. She observes her bent head, her inclined torso, her slumped shoulders, her hands folded in her lap clutching a damp handkerchief, and the way her body leans to the left. She looks at her dirty shoes and her wrinkled skirt, and despite everything she sees, she says, *Elena, I can't help you.* She says it calmly, as if she's been waiting for this moment her whole life, as if she'd prepared each word in advance. *I can't help you because I killed your daughter.* Elena's eyes open much wider than she thought they could, she begins to shake, and it's not Herself that makes her shake, but Isabel, the woman she set out in search of that morning who is now sitting across from her saying she killed her daughter. *I killed her by wishing her dead so many times,* Isabel clarifies, because she realises she needs to. *There hasn't been a single day in my life that I haven't wished to some god, some sorcerer, some star, that your daughter would die, and now she's finally dead.* Elena can't breathe, her drool flows freely, as if her saliva were her tears, she shakes, but she doesn't cry. *I'm sorry, I know you're her mother and I can imagine your pain, but it's not my pain. I killed your daughter but I will never go to prison for it, because I killed her with my thoughts. I killed her by wishing her dead so many times. I killed her without ever speaking to her again, without ever seeing her face to face. I killed her even if it was another person that put the rope around her neck, just like she killed me that afternoon she found me, locked me in her room. Do you remember that afternoon, Elena?* Elena says of course she remembers, she wouldn't be here if she didn't. *You have things wrong, Isabel, I don't understand what you're saying. We have different ideas of the debt that is owed, Elena,* she replies, *we don't even agree on who owes what. What are you talking about, then?* Elena asks as she wipes the handkerchief across her mouth and the last syllables of her words mix with the saliva and turn to paste. The two women fall silent for another moment, the cat moving between the two of them. Isabel stands up and turns on a lamp, which, Elena knows, was not necessary. *It's so absurd! All this time you've thought I felt indebted to your daughter; for twenty years you've believed something so different to what I believe. I've lived my life and you've lived yours, we've both constructed that past, that day, as if we weren't both there in the same place at the same time. It's absurd, yes,* Elena says, *Rita is relentless, was relentless, but thanks to my daughter's relentlessness you have your own daughter, you have to take the good with the bad.* Isabel cuts her off, *I never understood that saying, Elena, what's the good you're referring to? And does the good come because of the bad or the bad because of the good? You're mixing everything up again, you're confusing me, you're asking too many questions,* Elena says. *I didn't want to be a mother,* Isabel repeats the same words, twenty years later. *You thought you didn't,* Elena corrects her. *I never wanted it,* the woman insists. *You thought that before you held the baby in your arms, but once you had her in your lap, nursing at your breast, you.* Elena isn't able to finish her sentence because Isabel cuts her off again, saying, *I was never able to nurse her, my breasts were empty. I'm sorry,* Elena says. *Don't be sorry, I didn't want to be a mother, everyone else wanted it, my husband, his partner, your daughter, you, my body grew for nine months and Julieta was born, condemned to life with a mother who didn't want to be one,* the woman says. But Elena doesn't listen, *Until you saw her, now that she's here, living in your house, calling you Mum. She doesn't call me Mum, she calls me Isabel, she always knew, I didn't even have to say it. I did what I could, I fulfilled my duties, I fed her, I took her to school, I bought her clothes, I threw her birthday parties, I even loved her in a strange way, she's a good person, it's easy to love her. But I never loved her like she was my daughter. Her father did, he was both father and mother to her. He's the one who takes the pictures and sends them out every year, he and his partner, Julieta's godfather, who shares the clinic and other things with him. They're her parents. I'm something else, something that doesn't have a name, someone she cares about like you might care about a friend, or a neighbour or a roommate or travel companion. But that's all we are. Travel companions. I don't know what it feels like to be a mother because I'm not one; what does it feel like to be a mother, Elena, can you tell me?* Elena can't speak, she shakes like never before. She doesn't want to hear any more of what this woman has to say, levodopa, dopamine, Herself, the whore, Mitre, 25 de Mayo, Moreno, Banfield, Lanús,

123

Lupo, the Hippodrome, she repeats the names, changes the order, mixes up the words that no longer have any meaning, but over her confused prayer, she can hear what Isabel is saying, *I wasn't ever a mother even though you tried to force me to be one. It would be nice if now, after twenty years, you could finally get that through your head*. The woman walks over to the mantelpiece, picks up the framed picture of her husband and her daughter and she hands it to Elena. *This is all we are. A picture. A family portrait for other people to admire*. Elena looks at the picture that she's already seen, but she looks at it differently now, searching for signs of the truth. Maybe Isabel's smile in the picture is fake, or maybe her arms crossed under her chest show she's uncomfortable, or maybe it's significant that her gaze doesn't meet the camera, as if she looked up a second after the camera clicked, late because she had been in another place or another time. Elena sets the picture down on the couch and tries to stand but she can't. She wants to leave this house now that she knows she won't find what she's looking for. She wants to return home, retrace her route in reverse, Olleros, Libertador, Hippodrome, but she mixes up the order of the streets, she can't even stand, she shakes. Isabel walks over to her, *Do you need help? It's useless*, Elena answers, *I have to wait. Then wait*, the woman says. And Elena clarifies, *I'm going to have to wait here*. Isabel looks at her and then says, *We've already waited all these years*. They both fall silent once again. Elena knows that Isabel is looking at her, she knows what she's looking at. Elena observes the other woman in return, examines her legs, crisscrossed with little blue veins like spider webs. Isabel notices and moves them to the side. *Things turned out so differently*, Elena says. *Different to what? To what I always imagined, different to what made me come all the way to your house. I wouldn't have come if I'd known*. Isabel bends her head to look Elena in the

124

eye but Elena avoids her gaze. Isabel stands up and then says, *I'm not so sure, you might've come anyway. You confuse me*, Elena says, and she looks around the room although she doesn't know what she's looking for. Isabel sits back down. *That afternoon your daughter told me that if I had an abortion I'd hear a baby crying in my head for the rest of my life, but she hadn't had an abortion, she didn't know, she was repeating what someone else had told her, maybe a man, maybe not, but someone who thought they knew. I'd have liked to talk to your daughter before she died to tell her what I've heard in my head every day of my life since then, since that day she dragged me dizzy and vomiting to your house.* Elena, in spite of her confusion, makes an effort to listen, to follow what the woman is saying, she squints, concentrating on understanding the words, but she can only understand fragments as Isabel says, *I don't know what it feels like to have an abortion but I do know what it feels like to be a mother even though you don't want to be one, Elena. I know how it feels to have empty breasts, and the guilt when her tiny hand stretches for yours but you don't want to touch her, you don't want to rock her, or swaddle her, or warm her up or cuddle her, and the shame of not wanting to be a mother, because everyone, all the people who say they know what they're talking about, insist that a mother should want to be a mother.* The woman pauses to push her hair out of her face and wipe sweat from her brow. Elena squeezes her balled up handkerchief but doesn't offer it because she knows the rag she uses to wipe her drool isn't fit to be shared. *People like your daughter, who didn't even know me, your daughter who didn't have the nerve to become a mother herself but who treated my body as if it were hers to use, just like you, today, you didn't come here to settle a debt but to commit the same crime all over again twenty years later. You came here to use my body. I didn't*, Elena says. *Isn't that what you just said to me a few minutes ago? No, that's not why I came. But that's what you said. I don't know what I said. You should know. You confuse me. Why did you come to my house, ma'am? Say what you have to say once and for all, and then go.* Elena can't see Isabel's eyes but she knows that the woman is crying, she knows because of the way her legs are trembling. Elena gives her a moment. She stares at the carpet, Isabel's feet rubbing against each other, caressing themselves. Then she looks around for the cat but can't find it. She knows she should say something, clear up the misunderstanding, explain that she didn't come to commit any crime, that she has never in her life committed any crime, but she can't, she can't even think clearly. She doesn't know anything anymore. Isabel is the one who speaks first, repeating for the third time, now crying, the question that neither one of them has been able to answer so far, *Why did you come here today?* Elena repeats the words over and over inside her head to drown out the sounds of Isabel crying. She adds them to the tide of so many sobbed words, the king and the whore and the levodopa and the dopamine, and the streets backward and forward, but she messes it up, she knows she's left some out, that she's skipped over more than she wanted to, she starts over, repeats the prayer, she gets lost. She's thrown off by Isabel's crying, and now her questions, *How can you be so sure your daughter didn't commit suicide? Because it was raining, dammit! And my daughter was afraid of lightning rods, she was afraid of being struck by lightning, she would never have gone near a church on a rainy day.* But Isabel doesn't budge, *Never isn't a word that applies to our species, there are so many things that we think we'd never do and yet, when put in the situation, we do them.* Elena feels heat rise up through her body until her blood boils, she doesn't know what to do, what to say, or she does know, she thinks, she'd like to hit this woman sitting across from her, to grab her by the shoulders and shake her, and then look her in the eye and shout in her face to shut her up once and for all. But as much as she'd like to she can't. She can't even stand up and leave. She's stuck here, in this house, caught in the trap she set for herself, forced to listen to what Isabel has to say, like a curse. And thinking about the fact that her curse is unavoidable, that she is powerless, the heat gradually subsides, her body relaxes, and she is once again a stooped old woman, listening to what another woman has to say. Isabel dries her tears with her hands, and dries her hands on her skirt. She takes a deep breath to be sure she's not going to cry, and then she says, *I would've sworn that I'd never even have considered having an abortion, but I'd only thought about it, without ever having been pregnant, my decision was in my head, not in my body. I thought that before I'd ever had anything inside me. The day I did, when I went to get the test results and saw they were positive, it wasn't just something imagined anymore. For the first time, I knew.* Isabel looks at Elena, waiting for her to say something, but Elena can't, so Isabel continues, *People confuse thinking with knowing, they let themselves confuse the two. When I read the results and I saw it was positive, I knew that what I had inside me wasn't a child, and that I had to deal with it as quickly as possible.* Elena wipes her handkerchief across her face as if she were sweating too, she feels the damp cloth running over her skin. *They could've told you a dozen times what it feels like to have Parkinson's, in precise, graphic words, sparing no details, but you only knew the truth once the disease was inside your body. You can imagine the pain, the guilt, the shame, the humiliation. But you only know something once you've experienced it in your life, life is our greatest test.* Isabel stands and walks to the window, she looks outside, if Elena could see, she'd see a tree bursting with new green leaves but since she can't see, she just wonders what the woman is looking at. *You know, I was never in love with my husband, we were both virgins when we married and in the beginning I wasn't able to open up enough to make love with him, we couldn't do it. It wasn't until three months after getting married that we finally did it, and it was violent. He pulled my legs apart and said, you're going to open up, one way or another. I had bruises for several days, and pain, a pain that lasted a long time, it wasn't just that night, he kept it up until I got pregnant and then he never touched me again. It's been twenty years since he touched me. Does it bother you that I'm telling you this?* Elena thinks that Isabel's pain bothers her much less than her own pain but she doesn't say anything, she just makes a gesture with her hand for the woman to continue. *He goes out with his partner. They take trips together, they are companions. My husband named him Julieta's godfather. That's him in the picture on the mantelpiece.* Isabel walks to the mantel and picks up the photo, she looks at it for a moment and then takes it to Elena, to the couch she's confined to. Elena holds the frame and looks at it. *Him,* she says. The women fall silent once again. Elena doesn't know what to do with the picture she has in her hand, she searches for the other one, the one she looked at earlier, where Julieta's father had his arms around the two women, she stacks the two frames and she gives them to Isabel, who doesn't look at them, she just places them back on the mantel, in the exact same position and distance from one another as before. *The night my husband first took me by force, he was there, I didn't see him, the bedroom was dark, but I'm sure he was there, Marcos wouldn't have had the nerve on his own, he wouldn't have been able to. He was also here that afternoon you brought me home, when I begged you not to make me come in. He helped my husband keep me under control the whole nine months I was pregnant, they kept me almost like a prisoner, sedated, a nurse with me all day, as if I were crazy. They told me I was crazy, and there was another nurse at night, watching me sleep. They took care of everything and I let them do it. I've never been a strong woman, the one time I was able to muster*

128

any courage was that afternoon Rita found me at the place near your house. Elena remembers, *Who is this woman, Rita? Why did you come back? I heard a voice, Mum.* Isabel continues, *A nurse from my husband's clinic gave me the address. She saw me crying after I went to see him with the test results, she probably heard the shouting too. He already knew, the lab had let him know, the medical field is full of informants who work for people with power. I'd gone to beg him, to tell him I didn't want to have a child. He slapped me in the face, said he was ashamed of me, that he would divorce me right there if it weren't for what I had inside me. I went out into the hall, and I couldn't even walk so I sat down, and that's when the woman approached me, the nurse, and without saying anything she put a slip of paper in my pocket with an address and a name: Olga. I've never been a strong woman, all the strength I'd mustered I lost that afternoon you and I first met.* Elena is still shaking, Isabel moves closer to her and even though she doesn't say anything, her voice echoes inside Elena's head, asking, again and again, *why did you come?* Isabel's voice drowns out her own to the point that she can't even recite the streets that will take her back home. *One day, some day, like the day your daughter found me vomiting on the pavement, or the day your daughter was found dead in the church belfry, or today, life will test us. For real, not a dress rehearsal. And on that day we will finally realise that we are all alone, forced to face ourselves, with no lies left to cling to.* The woman goes to the window and straightens the curtain, unties the bow that holds it open and then reties it. Isabel looks at Elena, sitting there mutely with her head bent, unable to look her in the face. She moves closer, she sits beside her, and she waits. She will wait for as long as it takes for Elena to be able to say something. *It was raining,* Elena says eventually. Isabel doesn't allow herself to feel sorry for the woman. *No one's disputing the rain,* she says. *That's all I have. Then you have nothing. What do you want from me?*

Elena exclaims angrily, and Isabel replies *I don't want anything from you, you're the one who came to my house. You confuse me*, Elena says, *you make me mix everything up.* Isabel waits, she gives her more time and only when she thinks she's ready to listen she says, *I wouldn't have ever known I was capable of doing such a thing until my menstruation stopped and the lab test came back positive. What test could life have placed in front of your daughter to make her do something she never thought she'd do? What could've made her decide she didn't mind going to a church on a day like that? What could've been so terrible that she preferred to walk through the thunder and lightning she believed could kill her? Maybe she wanted the very thing she'd been so scared of before, for a bolt of lightning to split her in two. And when it didn't happen, when she got there and realised it was all a lie, that she was soaking wet but still alive, she chose to climb the tower, tie the kind of knot she'd never thought she knew how to tie, put the rope around her neck, and hang herself.*

3

Two days before she was found hanging in the belfry, Rita went to see Dr Benegas. Elena didn't know, he didn't tell her. He did tell Inspector Avellaneda after Rita died. Elena wanted to know what they talked about that day, but she hadn't thought it was important enough to ask, and now she's too far away to get answers. She does know what Rita talked to the doctor about two weeks before that, because she was there. It was the last time the mother and daughter saw Dr Benegas together, not in his office but at the hospital. He'd suggested that Elena should be admitted for a couple of days to do a battery of tests. *It's better to do it all at once, Elena, you don't want to have to deal with a lot of coming and going.* Elena was admitted, she brought two new nightgowns with her but she only wore one. She'd always kept new nightgowns on hand, ever since she found out she was sick. *In case I have to go into the hospital all of a sudden.* But even with two nights in the hospital she used just one, she doesn't know why. They took blood, did an MRI, tested her reflexes by tapping her knees, looked in her eyes, looked inside her with some machine or rays or something. But they looked, she knows that.

They made her walk, lift her arms, lower them, sit, stand. *Very good, María*, they said to her, because even though no one calls her by her first name her ID says María Elena and she was admitted under the name María E. but they ignored the E. They asked questions, *How long does it take for you to feel better after you take the pill? How long until it begins to take effect, María? And how long do the effects last?* They wrote down all her answers and took notes on what they observed. She was being treated by one of the best Parkinson's specialists in the country, Dr Benegas had told them, and his whole team, because the specialist didn't come alone but with an entire entourage, a group of ten residents who worked with him, proud to be a part of that medical school and to learn from him, and from her. Sometimes they came in twos or threes, to ask things they'd already asked, to take her blood pressure, or just to look at her. Sometimes they got the patients mixed up and asked her about some disease she'd never even heard of. Or they asked about symptoms she'd never suffered, and for a moment she would feel relieved, because if she didn't have those symptoms she couldn't be that badly off. Then, thanks to some chance question or comment, *Where's your husband today, Zulema?*, she'd realise they weren't talking about her, they'd gone into the wrong room, or picked up the wrong chart, or they were on the wrong floor or in the wrong wing. She was nice to them regardless, if anyone could help her it was these doctors, the more of them the better. But they didn't help her. After two days and countless tests, Dr Benegas came to give her the results. *Well, you know that Parkinson's and its evolution have to be studied clinically, there's no test that can definitively tell us that you have it, or how much you have it, or how far it has advanced, so we can only observe it clinically, do you understand?* The women didn't respond so Benegas continued, *Bearing that in mind, it's my duty to commu-nicate the information the team has gathered and share the conclusions they've reached. Tell us, Doctor*, Rita said. *I don't know if you, Elena, are going to want to hear it. Tell us, Doctor*, Elena said. *Your mother has a particular type of Parkinson's, what we call Parkinson-Plus, do you understand? Plus?*, Elena asked. *Extra, something more than your regular everyday Parkinson's*, Benegas clarified. *We did a whole battery of tests before reaching this conclusion, and we no longer have any doubts, it's Plus. Plus*, Rita repeated. *Yes*, the doctor confirmed. *Plus means more?*, Elena asked. *More?*, Rita said. *Yes, more. There's more, doctor?*, Rita asked again. *It seems so, child*, Elena answered. But Rita wasn't content with her mother's answer and she continued, *You think what we're dealing with isn't enough, Doctor? No, I'm not saying that, I'm saying there's more. And I, Doctor, am wondering if you know what you're talking about. Rita!*, Elena scolded. *You say there's more?*, her daughter asked, ignoring her and going on, *More than drooling, pissing herself and stinking of stale piss no matter how much you wash her, more than being unable to take a step on her own, more than dragging her feet the few steps she is able to take thanks to your levodopa, tell me: what more can there be, Doctor? Tell me!*, Rita repeated, and she glared at him until Benegas complied. *Rita, I think right now, in front of your mother, we shouldn't…* but he didn't get the rest of the sentence out before Rita interrupted him. *More than being forced to stare at the ground, condemned to spend the rest of her life with her head down like she's ashamed? More than being an unpleasant reminder to people who want to avoid seeing her? More? Rita, I understand, but this is not the time. No, you don't understand*, she assured him. *It's not the doctor's fault, child. It's not mine either, Mum. We'd better go*, Elena said, but Rita wasn't finished yet. *More than being unable to sit down or get up without help, to cut her own toenails, to tie her shoelaces? There's more? More than barely being able to swallow, barely able to breathe, thinking she's going to suffocate? More than eating with her hands, having to try a hundred times before she can pick up a pill, more than having to drink through a ridiculous plastic straw, more than not being able to pull her underwear up or down on her own, or wipe her backside after she takes a shit? That's enough, child,* Elena tried to silence her, but Rita wasn't listening to anyone but herself. *There's more, Doctor? More than not being able to button a blouse or put on a watch, or zip up her* handbag, *more than not being able to put in or take out her dentures, more than falling over if there's nothing supporting her torso, little by little, almost imperceptibly, until she's lying down on a park bench, leaning against who knows who, more than barely being able to sign her name or read her writing, more than her jaw being clenched shut so that she can't enunciate and you can only guess what she's trying to say? More? You're saying there's more, Doctor?* Dr Benegas tried to get a word in, *I'm going to have to ask you to...* but she interrupted him. *You don't have to ask me to do anything,* Rita spat as she stood up, placed her hands on the table and leaned over until her face was close to his. *Take a look, if you dare, into her dead eyes, into her expressionless face, her hollow smile, you're really going to ask this poor woman for more? Your mother is strong, you should be grateful for that. But what about me; what are you asking from me? Just that, Rita, a little more, I'm sorry but that's the way it is, it's going to ask more of you. What do you mean, exactly? Don't ask me to be more precise in front of your mother. I'm not asking it, I'm demanding it. I want to know, Doctor,* Elena said, *tell me what else it's going to ask of me. If that's what you want, Elena, I have the obligation to tell you everything I know: the disease will advance more quickly than we'd predicted, in a short time you may not be able to get out of bed, you won't be able to feed yourself, or go to the*

134

bathroom without help, you'll only be able to eat liquids or semi-liquid food, it will be impossible to understand your speech, you won't be able to read, it's likely that you might even experience symptoms of dementia, forgetting things, memory loss. You, Rita, are going to have to think about hiring someone to take care of your mother while you're at work, the sooner the better for the both of you. Time is short. Rita stood up and without taking her eyes off him, Are you saying she's going to die soon, Doctor? No, the issue at hand is not the amount of time but the quality of life. And what's the solution, Doctor? There is none, Rita, it's the hand she was dealt. It's the hand I was dealt, child, Elena said. The hand we were dealt, Mum, no cure, no solution, none. Rita stared at the doctor and then said, I can think of one solution, Doctor. What solution? You know. What are you referring to? Plus, you say, more, and if I can't take any more there's one thing I can do. I don't understand. A person can choose, Doctor. Not always, Rita. As long as a person's alive there's always hope, your mother is going to live, your mother wants to live. I want to live, child, Elena said. I'm not talking about my mother, said Rita, I'm not sure I'm going to be able to handle any more. You want to put me in a home, Elena said. No, Mum, not a home. Leave me on my own, don't take care of me if you don't want to, but leave me in my own house. You don't understand anything, Mum. You're going to be able to handle it, Dr Benegas said, you have to, for your mother. I want to stay in my own house, Rita, I can do it, child. Dr Benegas looked at Rita, There comes a time for us to give back what our parents gave to us, she needs you like you needed her years ago, you're going to have to be your mother's mother, Rita, because the Elena we know is going to be a baby. A baby, Rita asked, What are you saying, Doctor? Babies are cute, babies have soft white skin, and clear drool, a baby's body learns to sit and stand, one day it learns to walk, it gets new teeth, white and healthy. What my mother is going through is the exact opposite, instead of learning to control her sphincters she's pissing and shitting herself, instead of learning to talk she's going mute, instead of standing tall she'll become more and more hunched over, more and more defeated, and I'm condemned to watch as her body dies without her dying. Rita cried for the first time in a long time. *No, Doctor, my Mum's not going to become a baby, and I don't think I can become the mother you're asking me to become. We can provide help and support, Rita. For me or for her? Both. Here*, said Dr Benegas, picking up some pamphlets and holding them out to show the women. Rita wiped her tears from her face but she didn't touch the pieces of paper the doctor was trying to hand her so Elena leaned over, opened her palms, and waited for Dr Benegas to place them in her hands. *Thank you*, she said, gripping the flyers as best she could. Then she held her arm out so her daughter could help her stand, and they left.

They walked back home in single file, Rita in front and Elena several steps behind. Like when they'd had a fight. But they weren't arguing or whipping each other with their words. They didn't speak the entire way home. Rita walked slower than usual, but not slow enough for her mother to catch up. When they got home Rita locked herself in her room and Elena went to the kitchen to make dinner. She started heating water for some pasta, and waited. To pass the time while the water boiled she took the pamphlets from her handbag and called her daughter to come so they could look at them together, but Rita was in the shower and didn't respond when she shouted, so she began to read them on her own. Elena skipped over everything she already knew. She didn't bother to read the general description

136

of the illness or its symptoms, except for the ones she'd never heard of. Fish face or mask, caused by lack of expressiveness of the facial muscles. She strained to get a look at her reflection in the window that was starting to steam up from the cooking. If she had a fish face she hadn't realised it, and no one had told her. She pursed her lips like she was blowing a kiss and then opened and closed her mouth several times as if the fish that her face hid was breathing through its gills. Maybe she did have a fish face. Akathisia, inability to remain seated and still; that wasn't one of her symptoms, she could sit still. For now. Hypokinesia, that wasn't one of her symptoms either, she thought, but she kept reading and realised that while she'd never heard the word, she had experienced what it described: muscle rigidity. Constipation, sometimes, Dr Benegas's lazy intestines, but nothing that couldn't be solved with some stewed fruit or vegetables. She skipped the rest of the symptoms and moved on to the causes. She didn't care if what damaged the substantia nigra was a toxin or free radicals. She hadn't known fifteen percent of cases were genetic, but she couldn't remember anyone in her family who'd had Parkinson's. She moved on to some interesting facts, 'The name of the illness comes from James Parkinson, the English doctor who first described the illness in 1817, at the time he called it agitating paralysis'. She stopped to think about those verbs. Describing an illness. Observing it, looking at it in order to tell others about it, with all the contradictions that implied, like the contradiction of saying a paralysed body is agitated. She imagined someone trying to tell her about this illness that she now knows better than anyone because it's inside her. She could describe it better than Dr Parkinson, she thinks, and she'd call it Elena's Affliction. Or simply Elena's,

without any add-ons, like Parkinson's. She called for
Rita again before moving on to the Advice on How to
Deal with Symptoms, a pamphlet designed for sufferers
of the illness and their caregivers. But the water was still
running in the house's only bathroom, and Rita didn't
answer. So once again she started reading on her own, the
pamphlet talked about anxiety, depression, and distress,
in the patient as well as the person who had to take
care of them, called 'the caregiver'. That would be Rita.
It advised the caregiver to practice relaxation exercises
and breathing techniques that included repeating the
phrase 'let the tension flow out through my feet'. Or
breathing in and out for fifteen minutes repeating the
word 'calm' as if it were a mantra. Calm. Calm. She
thought a more accurate mantra would be shit, shit, shit.
She stood up to put the pasta in the water. She couldn't
rip the bag open with her hands so she stabbed it with a
knife, splitting the bag in half and spilling several pieces
onto the floor. She dumped the rest into the pot. She
returned to the table and picked up the last pamphlet,
Advice for Better Living. There were three categories:
Shared Activities, Activities Considered Achievements,
Enjoyable Activities. The pamphlet suggested that each
patient and caregiver make their own list and then
attempt two activities per day. She obediently made a
list in her head. She read the examples from the printed
list that had been included as a model. Exercise with
a friend, Go shopping, Go to the beach, Participate
in a play, Sing in a choir. She discarded them all for
her and Rita. There was no beach nearby, she'd never
exercised in her life, she hated spending money on
useless things, and would never get on a stage or sing in
public. She continued on to the Activities Considered
Achievements. Change a lightbulb, Write a poem, Build
a snowman, Solve a crossword puzzle. She added solve

a crossword to her mental list and wondered where this pamphlet had been printed, she'd never even seen snow, let alone touched it. She wondered if snow had a smell, like rain has a smell. Build a snowman. The shower stopped and Elena heard Rita's bedroom door open and then slam shut. She went to check on the pasta, which had started bobbing to the surface so she lowered the flame to minimum. She stood beside the burner for a few minutes until, without trying them, just by the colour and appearance, she guessed that the pasta had boiled long enough. She drained the pasta in the sink, a few drops of scalding water splashing onto her foot and burning her. She added to her mental list of achievements, drain pasta without splashing. She put some chunks of butter into a bowl and dumped the pasta on top then covered it with a dish towel so it wouldn't get cold. She went back to the table to continue reading. Enjoyable Activities: Go for a hike in the woods. No woods, no beach, no snow. Watch your favourite television show, she added that to her list. Read a book of jokes, Hug someone you love. Hug. She doesn't remember the last time she hugged someone or was hugged by someone. She can't remember.

Rita appeared in the doorway and said, without shouting, *You left the stove on, the house is going to burn to the ground*, and she walked into the kitchen but didn't turn it off, she just sat down in front of her empty plate at the table. In this position, Elena couldn't see that her eyes were red. She held out the pamphlets in front of her daughter, *Take a look at what Benegas gave us, child, there are some things that might...* but she didn't get to finish her sentence because Rita ripped the pamphlets from her hand. She held them for a moment, not reading them, just gripping them tightly and resting her vacant red-eyed gaze on the pamphlets she knew were useless. *That's enough, Mum, enough*, she said and she stood up, walked over to the stove, turned the flame to maximum, and set the pamphlets on fire. When the flame was about to burn her hand she let them fall, the charred pages fluttered to the green tile floor, landing beside the uncooked pieces of pasta that her mother had spilled.

Rita stood motionless watching the paper as it blazed, crackled, and danced until it changed colour, melted away, turned to ashes, and finally, went to the place that fire goes when it burns out.

4

Elena takes the pill she's supposed to take and waits, sitting on the couch in the house she set out for that morning, with a cat she just met sitting at her feet and a woman she only met one afternoon twenty years ago waiting along with her. She can feel the pill making its way down her throat; it's halfway there. She doesn't dare to speak out of fear that if she opens her mouth, the pill will move back up her throat and she'll have to start the whole process over again. Mute, she stares at the legs of the woman she set out in search of that morning and without saying a word she asks her for a few more minutes, enough time for the levodopa to dissolve and her body to be able to move, to retrace the route that brought her here. Isabel seems to understand her gesture or her gaze, saying, *Take all the time you need, I already told you I'm in no rush*. Elena closes her eyes and tries to remember the prayer she recites while she waits, but once again she's confused, she mixes up the words, she wonders if she'd be able to list the streets if she were alone, to remember the order of the ones she has to pass to get to the train that will take her home, and also the other ones, that she'll have to walk from the station to her house. Forwards and backwards and backwards and forwards, one, two, a hundred times, she wonders if she'll be able to say her prayer for the dethroned king and the naked emperor, the messenger and the whore; the sternocleidomastoid, the substantia nigra, the whore, and the levodopa. But she doesn't say her prayer because she's not alone and everything is all mixed up, and she gets nervous when she gets them out of order, and then the medication takes longer to have effect. She breathes, she has almost stopped shaking. The woman serves her another cup of tea and fabricates a new short straw out of the rest of the straw still on the tray the way she saw Elena do. She bends it, cuts it with the knife, puts it in the cup, then kneels down in front of her and puts the cup without its saucer between her hands. Elena takes it and even though she doesn't take a sip she nods her head as if saying thank you, and waits for the woman to move away, but Isabel doesn't move, she stays there, sitting on the floor next to the cat, so that she can look Elena in the eye, see her face to face. The pill finally completes its journey and begins to dissolve, freeing up Elena's mouth and throat to take a sip of tea and then say, *I loved her and she loved me, you know? I don't doubt it*, says Isabel. *In our own way, of course*, Elena clarifies, but the other woman doesn't need the clarification so she replies, *It's always in our own way*. The cat sitting between the two women meows. *Was I a good mother? Who can ever know?* Isabel pets the cat, and the cat twists, curves, leans into the caress, stretches to make it last longer. Elena watches them and holds out her hand to do the same thing but she can't reach, her hand hovers in the air, empty. She puts her arm back down beside her. *It was raining, she says. Even so,* the woman answers. *My daughter went even though it was raining. Your daughter went because it was raining and because there was something that scared her more than the rain. Me,* Elena says. Isabel looks at her, and

142

says, *Another person's body, sometimes, can be terrifying.* Elena holds out her hand again towards the cat, and this time the cat helps her by stretching its head towards her. The two women pet the same animal. *Do you think that Rita thought she was going to inherit my illness?*, she asks. *No, I think she couldn't stand that you had it. She never said that. Sometimes it's easier to shout than to cry. I'd have liked Rita to be here today, for her to have known,* Elena says. *She had to have known, in the end, when she felt that she couldn't go on living, after the shock and the disappointment, she must have known,* Isabel answers. The cat moves from one woman to the other, they share him. *I do want to live, you know? In spite of this body, in spite of my dead daughter,* Elena says, crying, *I still choose to live, is that arrogance? Not long ago I was told I was arrogant. Don't keep the names other people give you, Elena.* Isabel picks up the cat and puts it on her lap, Elena accepts it, she pets the cat and he curls up. *Do you like cats? I don't know,* Elena answers. *Well, we know the cat likes you,* the woman says. Elena smiles and cries at the same time, *He seems to like me, yes. What are you going to do now?*, Isabel asks, and Elena would like to have an answer, would like to say she's going to wait and then get up and leave, but so many words flood her head at the same time that they become tangled, overlapping, crashing into each other, and lose their way or disintegrate before Elena can pronounce them, so she doesn't say anything, she doesn't respond, because she doesn't know. Or because now she knows, she doesn't say anything, she doesn't respond, she just pets that cat. That's enough for today, petting a cat. Maybe tomorrow, when she opens her eyes and takes her first pill of the morning, she'll know. Or when she takes the second one. Maybe.

AFTERWORD

Claudia Piñeiro (born in 1960 in the town of Burzaco, Province of Buenos Aires, Argentina) is a key figure in contemporary Argentinian fiction, as well as a prominent and committed supporter of various high-profile campaigns including the successful legalization of abortion in Argentina, and the #NiUnaMenos movement against feminicide. She has also been active in trying to establish a writers' union in her country to give financial stability to the profession, and in 2019 she was named a Distinguished Citizen of Buenos Aires.

Her writing, which consists mainly of novels, but also a book of short stories, some fiction for young adults and collected plays, has won many significant awards: the Clarín Novel Prize for *Las viudas de los jueves* [*Thursday Night Widows*], the German LiBeraturpreis for *Elena sabe* [*Elena Knows*], the Sor Juana Inés de la Cruz Prize for *Las grietas de Jara* [*A Crack in the Wall*], the third National Literary Prize in Argentina for her most autobiographical work *Un comunista en calzoncillos* [A Communist in Underpants], the Rosalía de Castro Prize for her literary career, the Pepe Carvalho Crime Fiction Prize, and the Canadian Blue Metropolis prize for her work as a whole. *Elena Knows* was shortlisted for the International Booker Prize in 2022. In addition, four of her novels have been made into films: *Las viudas de los jueves, Betibú* [*Betty Boo*],

i

Tuya [*All Yours*] and *Las grietas de Jara*, and she wrote the script for a Netflix mini-series *El reino* [*The Kingdom*] with Marcelo Piñeyro, which launched in 2021 and immediately sparked controversy with its portrayal of the Evangelical church in Argentina.

Piñeiro has predominantly been presented to the English-speaking world as a crime fiction writer. To date, her novels in English translation have included *Thursday Night Widows, A Crack in the Wall, Betty Boo* and *All Yours*, all translated by Miranda France and published by Bitter Lemon Press. However, Piñeiro's status as the 'Queen of Crime Fiction', consolidated by the prestigious Pepe Carvalho prize, has perhaps overshadowed a broader appreciation of the urgent social scrutiny of contemporary society that her novels undertake. Pigeonholing her work as crime fiction downplays her critical gaze, which in recent novels has become ever more focused on pressing social issues. For Piñeiro, the solving of an individual crime is only half the story; a single crime often metonymically presents corruption at the core of society. As she put it on accepting the Pepe Carvalho Prize, 'crime fiction came into being to denounce injustice', and she claims that nowadays it is impossible to write a crime novel without also writing about the society in which the crime takes place. In 2018, she opened the International Buenos Aires Book Fair with a speech entitled 'What do people expect of a writer? Dissidence as a state of alert', and this sense of writerly responsibility for taking critical distance and tackling problematic social issues head on is an important aspect of her work. By bringing *Elena Knows* to an anglophone readership, Charco Press has relaunched Piñeiro in English as a writer of ethical weight and commitment.

Before analysing *Elena Knows*, a brief overview of her earlier novels helps to put it in context. The novel which shot Piñeiro to fame in 2005 was *Thursday Night Widows*, which focuses on four deaths in an exclusive gated community on the outskirts of Buenos Aires. Much of the novel revolves around the social circumstances of the families in the community, following the economic boom of the 1990s in Argentina, during which the peso was pegged to the dollar, though the narrative present is post-9/11 and the financial crisis. Who goes in and out of this community is strictly controlled, and when crimes are committed, a claustrophobic climate of fear and mutual suspicion sets in amongst the residents, whose usual tendency to obsessively compare themselves with their peers becomes unhealthily magnified. The novel's final provocative question, 'Are you afraid to leave?', as one family in crisis prepares to exit the dysfunctional social bubble, gently prods at the conscience of anyone who is living too comfortably in wilful ignorance of social division and breakdown around them.

Betty Boo has a similar setting to *Thursday Night Widows,* opening with a crime in a gated community, but here the investigative process takes centre stage. Piñeiro uses it to contrast old-fashioned investigative journalism with contemporary internet-based research and instant online news, alongside the exploration of criminal motives through fiction. She uses the novel to draw ethical conclusions about the need for individuals to weigh up conflicting news sources for themselves, making this novel feel very timely in the era of 'fake news'. *A Crack in the Wall* has an uninvestigated crime at its heart, but once again much of the plot is devoted to wider social scrutiny, examining the ways in which ideals of both individuals and institutions can become tarnished and behaviour compromised in a context of neoliberalist profit-driven practices. Furthermore, the presence of a buried body literally in the foundations of the building where the action takes place is used in the novel as a metonym for Buenos Aires' recent dark history, when during the 1976-83 military dictatorship political repression resulted in 'A city where so many of the dead lie outside the cemetery walls' *(A Crack in the Wall*, p. 188).

In *All Yours*, a superbly plotted and paced crime fiction novel, there is a secondary plot which competes for the reader's attention with the suspense of the main narrative. This subplot revolves around the question of access to clandestine abortion, and the consequences of the secrecy and taboos surrounding it for a middle-class family in which the parents are too self-obsessed to even notice that their daughter is pregnant. This emerging theme points clearly in the direction taken by *Elena Knows*.

Una suerte pequeña [A Little Luck] puts the main character Marilé into a crisis situation, where despite being a loving mother she feels she has no alternative but to abandon her husband and only son. Like many of Piñeiro's other works, the relationship between parent and child is examined in a state of maximum tension. *Las maldiciones* [Curses], for example, sees Piñeiro examine the nature of fatherhood. She also turns her critical gaze on politics, on how politics is conducted nowadays in the globalized, media-driven contemporary world, where policies are frequently shaped by what will secure the short-term popular vote, rather than by long-term objectives. In the collection of short stories *Quién no* [Wouldn't You], this cynical gaze alights on the world of bestsellers and moral bankruptcy in publishing in the stories 'La muerte y la canoa' [Death and the Canoe] and 'Bendito aire de Buenos Aires' [Blessed Air of Buenos Aires]; Piñeiro also returns her attention to the subject of abortion in 'Basura para las gallinas' [Scraps for the Hens], which focuses on two generations of women in a family passing on the painful knowledge of how to terminate a pregnancy with a knitting needle. This spotlight on women driven to take desperate measures, and on the hypocrisy and coercion of those around them, is at its most extreme in *Elena Knows*, which is Piñeiro's most sustained intervention, through the medium of fiction, in the long campaign to legalize abortion. (The novel's force can be likened to the impact of Portuguese visual artist Paula Rego's 1998 series of etchings of abortions, which were reproduced in Portuguese national newspapers in the days leading up to Portugal's second referendum on abortion in 2007.) It is perhaps for this reason that *Elena Knows* has not previously appeared in English: with this novel in particular, Piñeiro cannot be comfortably pigeonholed as (merely) a crime fiction writer; *Elena Knows* goes beyond its elements of crime investigation to raise urgent ethical questions, challenge religious hypocrisy and provoke reflection on myths of motherhood and maternal instinct.

Elena Knows

Elena is an unlikely heroine; an elderly Argentinian widow suffering from advanced Parkinson's disease whose relationship with her daughter Rita – who is also her full-time carer – frequently descends into mutual resentment and bitter argument. In spite of the title, rather than what Elena knows, the key to this profoundly moving novel is what Elena *doesn't* know. Piñeiro scrutinises their difficult mother-daughter relationship, using it to question to what extent women have control over their own bodies, and those of others. The story traces an arc from hubris to humility on Elena's part, and from conviction to despair on the part of her daughter, Rita, though this trajectory is masked by a non-chronological development. Their antagonistic relationship is triangulated with the life of

Isabel, who is also a mother, though she has lived a quietly tragic life rejecting that label.

Elena's biggest assumption is that as a mother, she knows her daughter, knows her fully and fundamentally, and therefore knows how she would react in any given circumstance. 'No one knows as much about her daughter as she does, she thinks, because she's her mother […] Motherhood, Elena thinks, comes with certain things, a mother knows her child, a mother knows, a mother loves. That's what they say, that's how it is.' (p. 49)

Elena's dogmatic insistence launches her on a painful journey towards self-knowledge, towards unlearning what she thought she knew, and to the realization that she did not, in fact, know her daughter as well as she thought. The journey is simultaneously exacerbated and propelled by Elena's suffering from Parkinson's disease. The fierce limitations that Parkinson's imposes on her world, both physically and mentally, are compellingly drawn; Elena cannot move without the aid of medication and her perspective is limited by the inability to raise her head beyond a certain point. 'Her time is measured in pills' (p.70), we are told, and the narrative reinforces this, being divided into three parts, 'Morning', 'Midday' and 'Afternoon', the times for Elena to religiously take the second, third and fourth pills of the day. This ritual, like a vestigial echo of monastic offices, is enhanced by Elena's personal litanies of repeated street names while she waits for the pills to take effect. Poignantly, we are left to speculate at what lonely point in the early hours, prior to the start of the narrative, Elena took her first pill of the day. Although not strictly observing unities of time, place and action, the three-part structure and intensity feels like a gesture towards Greek tragedy. The central plot takes place in the present, the single drawn-out day of Elena's arduous journey to see Isabel, although it is fleshed out by flashbacks to the events of twenty years before. The setting gravitates around the local neighbourhoods of Elena and Isabel in Buenos Aires, and there is a sense of unity of action in that the whole novel stems from a single decisive intervention by Rita which had devastating and long-lasting consequences for them all.

Societal forces are at work here which constrain the life choices of these three women. The Catholic church and its dogmas loom large, with its categorical statements about humans and their bodies: 'The Church condemns […] any wrongful use of the body that does not belong to us, whatever name you want to give the action, suicide, abortion, euthanasia.' (p. 53) Piñeiro explores these so-called 'wrongful' uses, giving a characteristic twist and creating many ironic parallels between her characters and the way their bodies use and are simultaneously used by others. Rita is seen to rigidly accept the church's doctrines to the extent of imposing them on a stranger, preventing Isabel from having the abortion she desperately wants; indeed Rita and her middle-aged boyfriend Roberto are 'united by their convictions […] about how another person should experience something they themselves had never experienced' (p.88). Yet Rita's body in turn is submitted to a painful and humiliating gynaecological examination, instigated by her mother and the medical establishment, to check if she has a womb and is fit for female purpose, and she later submits her own body to one of the church's 'wrongful uses' by committing suicide. Elena, meanwhile, suffers terribly at the hands of 'Herself', the 'fucking whore illness' (p. 3) as she resentfully calls her crippling Parkinson's disease, yet she fully intends to (ab)use Isabel's healthy body as a surrogate to carry out her own investigations into Rita's death.

Of all the characters, Isabel is the real victim; her body is assaulted from all sides, by her husband, by Rita, and (almost) by Elena.Yet as the tragedy unfolds, there is genuine resolution between her and Elena, as both women come to realise that *not knowing*, and not fitting into neat categories, is something that they share. Isabel, despite having a daughter, disavows motherhood saying 'I'm something else, something that doesn't have a name' (p. 123), and Elena doubts her success as a mother and even her right still to be called one, now that her only child has taken her own life, unable to face caring for a mother with Parkinson's. In the cinematic closing scene, the two distressed women tacitly bond over a substitute object of affection, Isabel's cat, who goes back and forth silently between them.

The issues raised by *Elena Knows* are universal, timely and complex: the obstacles to a woman's right to control her own body, the myths and realities surrounding motherhood, the mental and physical constraints on women's daily routines, the increasing challenges of an ill and ageing body. Although the issue of abortion is undoubtedly the central and burning theme of the novel, *Elena Knows* also asks the reader to put themselves in Elena's unenviable place of age and infirmity. One of the most moving moments in the novel occurs when Elena leaves an appointment after receiving her disability certificate. Roberto sees she is crying and asks why, to which she simply replies 'They treated me kindly' (p. 83). In this moment of vulnerability, we gain a rare insight into Elena's habitual brusqueness and forcefulness, which is revealed – at least in part – to be a necessary self-defence against the all-pervasive ageism and sidelining of elderly and disabled people on the part of society at large.

Elena Knows thus challenges fixed ideas on ageing, on disability and, above all, on abortion, and in her more recent novel, *Catedrales* [Cathedrals], Piñeiro dramatizes even more forcefully the potentially tragic effects of a rigidly traditional Catholic standpoint on abortion. *Catedrales* was published during the global lockdown resulting from the Covid-19 pandemic, and in a context of fierce public debates in Argentina around the legalization of abortion, which was eventually approved by the National Congress on 30th December 2020. Its powerful multi-voiced narrative, with each chapter told from the perspective of a different character, imagines the horrific lengths that a family member will go to in their misguided desire for 'decency' and preserving family honour.

In all of her work, Piñeiro does not shy away from the most pressing ethical questions. She places her characters in crisis situations where they have to take radical decisions; often her characters find that they do not truly know their own mind until their body is in peril, and at the crucial moment a deeper kind of knowledge emerges. *Elena Knows*, together with *Catedrales*, is perhaps the most deeply felt of Piñeiro's novels in its ability to tap into the raw emotion and extreme feelings surrounding the abortion debate, whilst presenting the reader with an elderly detective-heroine who is light years from the likes of Agatha Christie's Miss Marple: an objectionable and outspoken woman suffering advanced Parkinson's who stubbornly persists against the odds in investigating the death of her own daughter. In choosing to re-launch Claudia Piñeiro in English with this particular novel, Charco Press presents the author at her most committed, taking the tropes of crime fiction into a deeper ethical dimension and demonstrating supreme moral integrity. In creating Elena, Piñeiro offers us a truly extraordinary example of resilience, perseverance and – ultimately – willingness to change. Let us accept her gift.

Dr Fiona Mackintosh
University of Edinburgh
March 2021

CHARCO PRESS

Director & Editor: Carolina Orloff
Director: Samuel McDowell

www.charcopress.com

Elena Knows was published on
90gsm Munken Premium Cream paper.

The text was designed using Bembo 11.5 and ITC Galliard.

Printed in November 2023 by TJ Books
Padstow, Cornwall, PL28 8RW using responsibly
sourced paper and environmentally-friendly adhesive.